4 Ounces to Heaven
A Search for the Energy of Life

4 Ounces to Heaven

4 Ounces to Heaven
A Search for the Energy of Life

by Thomas Stirr
Author of *MILLER'S BOLT: A MODERN BUSINESS PARABLE*

Thomas-Ritt Associates Limited
P.O. Box 20055
1 Main Street West
Grimsby, Ontario L3M 5J3
CANADA

Email: info@4ouncestoheaven.com

Stirr, Thomas
4 Ounces to Heaven: A Search for the Energy of Life / Thomas Stirr
ISBN 0-9689831-0-3

Printed in Canada.

Jacket design by Thomas Stirr.

Graphic composition by Crawford Graphics, Burlington, Ontario Canada

First printing, November 2001.

THOMAS STIRR

For my wife Rosemary,
and our three children; Adam, Eric, and Erin.

May we all continue to love and learn
as we continue on our journeys

Do not look to the earth as your father,
for it did not deposit the seed of your life.

And it is not your mother,
for it did not open its womb to you.

A surrogate, the earth is not.
It is but a point of entry, a conduit that joins one energy realm to another,
linking paths of discovery and wonder before you.

There need not be pain, or fear, or jealousy, unless you choose it.
Cast away the crutch of yearning and reap
the bounty that is Now.

Take comfort in being lost and alone
and do not seek self-creation,
lest it hide you more.

Thomas Stirr
© Copyright 1996

4 Ounces to Heaven

Follow then the shining ones,
the wise, the awakened, the loving,
for they know how to work and forebear.

GAUTAMA BUDDHA

FOREWORD

There comes a time in everyone's life that the haunting question of "Why am I here?" dwells weightily as we strive to address many of the lessons created by our very existence. In that time we are drawn, often without knowing, to stories and storytellers that reflect for us the deeper rumblings in our souls.

The dawning of the Third Millennium has brought many choices to the human race. Our personal worlds have expanded and now are touched by the follies and foibles of people and circumstances unimaginable only a short memory ago. The expansion of our universe comes with the contraction determined by its natural cycle, and as we move further out we are forced to look further in. This is the natural way.

We are each represented in the world by the choices we make, and as humans our eternal search is for meaning. Every now and then a story comes along that reflects for us the magic of the search and the elation of discovery. The choices we are charged to make as a consequence of allowing new messages into our lives determine the next message that is destined to appear on our path. The question inevitably arises. Will we choose to expand our universe or contract our existence? On some things we can be sure, the messages will keep coming and our souls will continue to rumble.

4 Ounces to Heaven from master storyteller Tom Stirr will cause readers to feel emotions normally felt only when we look closely into the eyes of those we love, touch the hand of the one who makes us feel safe, or be in the presence of someone we know makes a difference just by being on this spinning orb. It is a story that reflects the power of the only choice we really have, Love or Fear.

Peter Comrie
President,
Glasshammer Communications Group

THOMAS STIRR

ACKNOWLEDGEMENTS

Special thanks to:

Peter Comrie for unwavering friendship and encouragement.
Dr. Paul Cano for clarifying medical terms and procedures.
Barry Siskind for help along the road called serendipity.
Ginette Doucette for cosmic connections.
Ted Light for insights and support.
Helen Spinney for proofreading

Thanks to a host of friends for their faith and support:

Tim Corrin, Chris Wheaton, Shelley Lynes, Tim Pennal, Morgan Comrie,
Kathy Penner, Michael Mangialardo, Mike Cook, Wayne Costello,
Eric Zahrai, Dave van Sickle, Tom Coffey, Christina Menard-Famili,
Doug Bolger Sr., John Eaton, Curtis Harren, George deLure, Lynda Harvey,
Neil Phillips, Larry Boychuk, Rob O'Dowda, Richard Kinch, Bill Kent,
Judy Harman, Deb Carlson, Dave Dunn, Jim Beiderweiden, Dave Kemp,
Dave Fisher, Terry Manion and Bruce Gordichuk.

CHAPTER 1

Laura Snider paused in the doorway, her eyes scanning the room. The left side was dimly lit by a row of antique wall mounted fixtures. Sprinkled on the tables throughout the room small candles flickered in honey-coloured glass containers casting grotesque shadows on the faces clustered around them. The voices in the room mixed, forming an unintelligible muffle.

A large, ornate bar with a brass foot rail running along its perimeter dominated the centre of the room. Wine glasses and brandy snifters hung upside down on overhead wooden tracks above the island serving area. Light from the serving area spilled out into the room and illuminated all the tables immediately adjacent to the bar.

Laura's heels clicked as she made her way to a corner stool at the bar, turning many of the heads as she passed. Snider placed her purse on the bar and hooked her heel on the barstool brace, the muscles in her thigh and calf flexing as she slid up onto the seat. She smiled as the bartender approached.

"Good evening Todd. You haven't been around for a couple of days."

"Missed me did you? I work part time so my shifts are sort of irregular," he replied.

"I'll have one of your special low octane Caesars."

"I see we have a woman of special tastes. One virgin Caesar coming right up."

As Todd prepared her drink Laura casually glanced down and opened her purse, taking out a package of cigarettes and a small, gold-embossed lighter. After lighting a cigarette, her gaze became more deliberate as she assessed the men at neighbouring tables. "Fat polyester," she thought. The clink of a glass being placed in front of her brought Laura's attention back to Todd. "What's happening at the hotel the next few days?" she asked.

"Typical week. We've got a couple of conventions starting today. The small one is in for three days. The other one goes five and ends on Saturday night," he replied.

"Small town types?"

"Yeah, pretty much. I'm not sure of the association names, but I'm reasonably sure both groups are made up of independent business owners. Hardware dealers and some kind of fast food franchise operation I think," said Todd, "Do you want to run a tab?"

Snider wrinkled her nose. "Don't think so." She reached into her wallet and pulled out a ten-dollar bill. "Will this cover it with a tip?"

Todd winked, "You bet."

Laura snapped her wallet shut, putting it back in her purse, then crossed her legs allowing the fabric of her dress to gently ride up, away from her knee. She cupped her drink and let her gaze drift from table to table. Within a few minutes a heavy-set man left his table and approached the bar, standing five or six feet away from Laura, and motioned to the bartender. Todd came over to take his order.

"Hey sport, rum and coke. Make it a double."

Todd nodded and wheeled back toward the serving area to prepare the drink. The waitress who had been serving the heavy-set man approached Todd, whispering to him and handing him the bar tab in her hand. The heavy-set man watched Todd and the waitress then shifted his gaze onto Laura Snider. He studied her as she sipped her drink, noticing the faint smudge of lipstick on her glass. His gaze traced the lines of her gold necklace then followed the pendent suspended from it down to the fullness of her breasts. His eyes widened as he studied her trim waist and the contours of her leg. Light from the serving area danced on a small, gold chain around her ankle.

"Should I add this to your tab?" Todd asked as he placed the double rum and coke down on the bar counter in front of the heavy-set man.

"Yeah, sure." replied the man his eyes still glued to the glitter around Snider's ankle.

Laura continued to scan the room slowly, her gaze eventually falling on the heavy-set man. She studied him casually then returned to her drink.

The man drank deeply from his glass and edged closer. "Are you in town for a convention?" he asked.

Snider smiled, "No, I don't go to many conventions. How about you? Is that what brings you to town?"

"Yeah. I'm with the independent hardware dealers' group. We're here for the next four days."

"So, is this something you do every year?"

"Not every year. My partner and I take turns. This year I happened to luck out. Our company has been a member of the association for the past eighteen years."

"Eighteen years. A lot of small businesses don't last that long. You and your partner must do a good job running things. Business going well?"

"No question we do well. But we have to keep that from the folks in town. You know what I mean."

"I understand. Business issues need to be kept strictly confidential. Do you come to Chicago very often? It's a such terrific city."

"No, this is actually my first trip to Chicago. Just never got around to coming up here before. Usually the association holds the convention in smaller cities in the mid-west. Kansas City. St. Louis. Omaha. That sort of thing. I'm really looking forward to the sessions tomorrow. There's always lots of new things to learn."

Laura stroked the salted rim of her glass with her index finger. "My mother used to say that if you have a good attitude a person can learn just about anything." She casually licked the salt from the tip of her finger. "Don't you just love the spices they put in these drinks?"

The sides of the heavy-set man's neck became flushed. He cleared his throat. "What brings you to Chicago?" he asked.

Snider smiled and extended her hand. "I guess it's kind of

rude to carry on a conversation without being introduced. Hi, my name's Laura."

The man shook her hand gently. "I'm Gary. Pleased to meet you Laura." He looked at her half-empty drink. "Would you like another?"

"No, I think I can nurse this one a while longer," she replied.

Gary motioned for a refill then turned back to Snider. "So what line of work are you in, Laura?" he asked.

"Well, I'm an independent businesswoman. I have my own personal services company."

His neck reddened further. "That's interesting. What kind of services do you provide?"

Laura's elbow was on the counter, her head tilted and cradled in her palm. She looked directly into Gary's eyes as she replied, "I've found there's a wide range of services an industrious woman can offer. The most important thing is to cater to the specific needs of my clients. Like my mother said, you can learn to do just about anything."

"How's business been?" he asked.

"Just like your business Gary. Things have been very good. I've found that the keys to success are to offer outstanding service, select your clientele carefully, and make sure you follow all appropriate safety precautions. If you do, you can build a very lucrative and enjoyable career," replied Snider.

"Do you have to travel much?"

"No, I'm not on the road much at all. I have a very loyal base of very exclusive clients that keep me busy and close to home."

"So, is this one of your road trips?"

"Not really. It's more of a working holiday," she replied.

Small beads of sweat started to appear on Gary's forehead as he felt his hands growing cold and damp. "Any chance I could fit into your holiday plans?"

Laura took a couple of sips from her drink then rotated in her seat so that her leg was pointed directly at Gary. "I suppose we could talk about that," she answered, "But not here."

Gary downed the rest of his drink and motioned to Todd, "Close me out, sport." After paying his tab he and Laura walked out of the bar toward the elevator, holding Todd's gaze as they left.

Laura made sure that her trip to the elevator with Gary was filled with small talk, purposely slowing down her gait so that she and Gary could enter an elevator alone. As soon as they were inside she pressed the 'Close Doors' button and held it in place.

"I think this is a good place for us to talk, Gary."

He looked at her quizzically.

"These days a woman can't be too careful." She studied him for a few moments. "What kind of personal service are you interested in?"

"Well, I kind of thought we could play that by ear. You know, once we were upstairs."

"That's no problem. I pride myself on being, shall we say, a flexible and accommodating person. It's not that I don't trust you Gary, but I need to see what you're packing down there," said Snider as she motioned to Gary's groin.

"What? Here? You want me to whip it out in here?"

Laura shrugged her shoulders and smiled, "Sure, why not? I'm holding the elevator door closed so this will be our little secret. I can't really take this issue any further with you until we get this over with. It's your move Gary. I need you to show me your equipment voluntarily. Once we get past this little test we can go upstairs and continue our discussion. You still want to go upstairs don't you?"

Gary nodded his agreement.

"I'd hate to think that you were a police officer Gary. You need to show me your equipment before we can talk any further. That way it would be entrapment if you were an undercover cop and tried to charge me with something later on."

Gary paused for a few seconds, his eyes running over Laura's body. Finally his hands went down to his belt. After undoing it, Gary unfastened the metal clasp and inside tab button on his suit pants. Then he lowered his zipper and reached into his underwear.

Snider glanced down to his groin. "Very nice." She then looked him in the eye, "Gary, I need you to clearly understand that I only deal with responsible clients, safety precautions are mandatory."

"That's okay with me."

"Good. The other thing you need to understand is that if we go upstairs and we play this by ear as you suggested, it will cost a little more."

"How much?" asked Gary as he did his pants back up.

Snider studied him for a moment then replied, "Three-hundred and fifty."

"Three-fifty? In Wrightsville it would only be a hundred."

Laura put on her best pout, "Gary, this is Chicago, not Wrightsville." She glanced at the control panel. "If we agree on three-hundred and fifty I can press floor number seven and you can find out about the very special services I offer to my customers. Otherwise I'll have to open the doors and let you go back to the bar."

Gary bit his lower lip, and wiped his palms against his suit jacket. "Okay. Three-hundred and fifty it is."

A demure smile crept over Laura's face as she calmly pressed the seventh floor button.

She studied Gary intently as they road the elevator to the seventh floor. His gaze was locked on the outline numbers lighting up above the door. As the elevator came to a stop she hooked her arm under his and led him down the hall to her suite. Once inside she motioned to the mini-bar.

"Gary, why don't you pour yourself a drink while I freshen up. By the way, what's your favourite colour?"

"Blue, I suppose," he replied quizzically.

"Let me see what I can do. See you in a few minutes," replied Laura as she retired to the bedroom.

Gary poured himself a Scotch. He paced nervously back and forth in front of the sofa, then walked to the window and looked out to the street below. His groin felt flushed and heavy. "Three-fifty!" he thought. "What the hell am I doing? This better be worth it." Gary heard movement coming from the bedroom area and turned to see Laura entering the room. She was dressed in a black lace bra; high cut panties, garters, stockings and spike heels. A thick, silver choker gleamed around her neck. She held a small, silver box in her hand. She casually picked through its contents as she spoke. "You said you liked blue," said Laura as she looked at Gary, "That's right isn't it?"

Gary nodded.

"Light blue or dark blue?"

"I dunno. Dark blue I guess."

"Why don't you sit down on the edge of the sofa," she cooed. Gary obeyed her command and watched as she removed a package from the silver box, and opened it up in her hand. He felt his pulse rising as she showed him the contents of the package, a navy blue condom that she held between her thumb and index finger. "I have some darker blue ones if you don't like this colour."

Gary cleared his throat, "No, that looks just fine."

Snider nodded her head. "Well Gary, it's time we get you fitted with some protection." Her gaze fell down his body, and lingered on his groin. She could feel his tension rising as she lifted her head and stared into his eyes. Smiling, she placed the unwrapped condom in her mouth and walked toward the edge of the bed.

CHAPTER 2

Just before Todd's shift ended Laura Snider reappeared in the bar. Even when dressed casually she looked spectacular; tailored blue denim pants with matching jacket, heels, and a white silk blouse open to mid-chest. A choker of scarlet beads flashed around her neck. Large scarlet earrings in the shape of treble clefs added a whimsical quality to her outfit.

"What can I get you?" Todd asked.

Laura studied his muscular frame for a few moments before answering, "I don't need a drink. What time are you off?"

Todd glanced at his watch, "About another fifteen minutes."

Snider flashed a wide smile, her eyebrows flicking upward. "That's great! This little girl has finished work for the day and is looking for someone to celebrate with tonight. Interested?"

"Could be. What did you have in mind?" replied Todd.

"Well, you must know an awful lot of people being a bartender."

"Yeah, sure I do."

"And, I imagine some of them might be pretty resourceful."

"Resourceful. That's an interesting choice of words," Todd said, "What are you looking for?"

Snider placed both of her elbows on the bar and leaned forward as she cooed, "A good looking guy who's into funky music, funkier women, and a little bit of snort."

"Can't help you with the snort," he said, "Why do you need that anyway?"

"Because it makes me feel so good after a hard day working," replied Laura.

"Maybe you shouldn't work so hard."

She studied him for a few moments then frowned slightly. "Well, you're a bit of a surprise. I had you pegged as a party guy, not a prude. I'm sure there's lots of guys in Chicago that could help a pretty girl like me have a good time."

"Only about a million."

"So what's the problem?"

"Hey look, if an out-of-the-way neighbourhood eatery and a secret little blues club appeal to you I'm available. I just don't get my kicks by using chemicals."

"And what kind of food would this neighbourhood eatery serve?"

"Chicago's best deep dish pizza and bruschetta you could die for."

"Mmm. Haven't had a great pizza in years. You said a blues club?"

"One where all the greats come to jam after they're done with their paid gigs in the city."

"What's the name of this place?"

"Now, if I told you that it wouldn't stay a secret would it?" Todd said smiling, "And, you wouldn't need me to take you there."

"Okay Todd, you're on", said Laura, "This evening isn't quite what I had planned, but it's not every day a girl gets to go to a secret blues club."

"Do you want to stay here until my shift's done and I change, or do you want to meet me in the lobby at a quarter after nine?"

"Make me a martini and I'll wait here."

"Olive?"

"Sure."

Todd mixed Laura her drink then served the other customers at the bar. Just after nine his replacement arrived. Todd hurried off to the staff room and returned to the bar, depositing six dollars in the cash register to pay for Laura's martini.

"Ready for pizza?"

"Mountains of it."

Laura hooked her arm around Todd's as they walked out of the lobby to his car. A cold blast of winter air greeted them as they left the hotel, causing an instant shiver to run through her.

"Chicago's the place to come if you want to remember what winter's like," she quipped.

"It's not that bad once you get used to it."

"So is this when you give me some line about it being a dry cold?"

"Nope. Cold is cold," said Todd as he breathed in deeply. "Even with the Chicago smog mixed in a crisp night like this really makes me feel alive." Dodging traffic they crossed the street to the parking lot. 'Watch your step," said Todd as he opened the car door for Laura.

"Chivalry isn't dead I see."

"It's one of my little quirks."

The car moaned its displeasure as Todd tried to start it. After two sputtering attempts it started. He put it in gear and eased out of the parking spot. "The adventure begins," he said as the car lurched out into traffic. Forty minutes later they arrived at the restaurant. It was just before ten, but the establishment was still bustling with activity. The owner, Tony Ambruzzo, greeted them as they entered.

"Ah! So, one of the Irishman's sons returns! And, he brings a lovely lady." Ambruzzo's outstretched arms embraced Todd warmly. "And who is this treasure?" asked Tony as he kissed Laura's hand.

"A special friend, Tony."

"Well, any friend of an O'Brien boy is always welcome here."

Ambruzzo escorted them to their table. As Tony left Laura couldn't help but grab Todd's forearm. "He's wonderful! Like a caricature of life! The flowing gray hair. That huge handlebar moustache. The red and white checkered apron. I thought people like that only existed in the movies, or in television commercials."

Todd smiled, "Tony's better than any movie character you could imagine. He's got a heart bigger than the city."

"How did you meet him?"

"Years ago my dad used to walk this beat..."

"Your dad was a cop?"

"Yeah, he got killed almost twenty-five years ago. I was a teenager when it happened. It was tough on my mother. She had to work two jobs to try and make ends meet. Tony gave my two brothers and me jobs in this restaurant. It helped to keep us off the street and out of trouble. The extra money helped keep the family together."

"He must have had a special relationship with your parents to do that."

"With my dad actually. When Tony came over here from Italy his dream was to have his own restaurant. He worked construction and lots of other jobs to save the money to open this restaurant. Within a month of opening this place up some local thugs tried to shake him down. Tony refused to pay protection money so they beat him up pretty badly. My dad was the first cop on the scene. Tony didn't back down at all and told my dad who beat him up and pressed charges. It never went to trial since the three of them eventually plea bargained the attempted extortion and assault charges."

"Tony sounds like a brave man."

"More than brave, Laura. He didn't back down even after he received death threats after the charges were laid. Tony told my dad that he wasn't going to let anybody scare him away from his dream. My dad really respected him and found Tony's determination and love of life inspiring."

"How did your dad die?"

"During the investigation my dad got to know Tony really well and they became good friends. My dad used to drop in frequently to chat. A few months after they were paroled, two of the thugs that tried to shake Tony down came back looking for him around closing time. My dad had just finished his shift and was visiting the restaurant. He was in the back helping Tony's wife in the kitchen when my dad spotted the thugs through the window in the kitchen door. He recognized them immediately, and expecting trouble, he drew his service revolver. As they showed their weapons my dad called out to them from the kitchen. A gun battle broke out, wounding Tony and the two thugs. My dad took three bullets in the chest and died in Tony's arms."

"I'm so sorry."

Todd looked up at her, "Tony promised my dad that he'd look out for us. He's been doing that faithfully for nearly twenty-five years."

"How about your mother?"

"She's still in Chicago. Never remarried. She likes to spend her time doting over my brothers' kids."

"And you?"

Todd smiled, "Kids you mean? I don't have any that I'm aware of. Enough about me. What about Laura? I don't even know your last name."

She shrugged her shoulders. "Not much to tell. Small town mid-west family named Snider moves to California when their daughter is in grade school. Daughter spends uneventful years at high school. Goes to college. Graduates. Falls in with fast crowd. Loves the good life; clothes, cars, chemicals. Works hard to get what she wants."

A smile broke on Laura's face as she looked over Todd's shoulder. Tony Ambruzzo was dancing over with a heaping plate of bruschetta and a pitcher of beer.

"Hope you don't mind," said Tony as he placed the plate and frothing pitcher, along with two frosted mugs on the table, "O'Brien's only drink beer with Tony's food."

"How could we go wrong with frosted mugs!" chimed Laura.

"Has Todd talked you into an O'Brien special yet?" asked Ambruzzo.

Laura's gaze was locked on Tony. Her elbows were on the table, hands clasped and cradling her chin. "An O'Brien special. Now, what could that possibly be?" she asked.

"Starts with double cheese, then…anchovies, spicy sauce, ham, bacon, hot sausage, onions, mushrooms, tomato slices, and that special O'Brien ingredient…calamari!"

"Squid? On pizza?" Laura looked at Todd with feigned disgust.

"Hey, it's a family tradition!" he replied in self-defense.

Snider gave Ambruzzo a wink, "Sounds great Tony."

Ambruzzo's smile widened. The tips of his moustache strained to touch his ears. "This will be a work of art!" he exclaimed.

They both laughed as Ambruzzo went dancing off toward the kitchen.

"Now there's a man who loves what he does," said Laura.

"This is a really special place for me. Whenever I need to put things in perspective I come and spend time with Tony. Being around him confirms what life's about."

"And what's that?"

"For Tony it's living every day to the fullest. I need that reminder from time to time." O'Brien scanned the room, "Coming here brings back good memories of all the help Tony gave me as a kid. It confirms the importance of giving to others, and having the courage to discover yourself, understand yourself, and be yourself. Being around someone like Tony lets me know how lucky I am to be here on this planet, and how special it is when I'm able to help others on their journey of discovery."

"That sounds pretty heavy for a bartender."

Todd smiled, "Yeah, maybe so. I suppose it depends on what you see when you look at people."

"What do you see when you look at me?"

"A contradiction."

Laura's lips drew tight. "Are you going to try and get me wrapped up in one of those 'how does a good girl turn bad' talks?"

Todd made direct eye contact with her, "Not for me to judge."

"Oh, I see. And you're not self righteous either!"

"Hey, where did that come from?"

"My experience with do-gooders."

Todd burst out laughing, "Hey calm down a little! All I want is squid pizza, a beer, and some friendly conversation."

Laura's eyes burned into him, "Yeah, sure."

Suddenly Todd sprang up from his chair and screamed, "Tony! Tony! We need a song!"

The restaurant went silent with everyone gawking at Todd. Suddenly the swinging doors to the kitchen flew open. Laura turned to see Tony burst from the kitchen with a pizza tray over his head, spinning around several times, then breaking into song, "When the moon hits your eye like a big pizza pie...that's amore!"

Todd danced across the floor toward Tony. She watched as they held each other around the waist, twirling between tables singing in unison. At the end of their song the patrons applauded loudly. Todd held Tony's head in his hands and kissed him on the cheek. Tony slapped him on the back and pushed him towards Laura.

"Go you young fool! You should not waste time with an old man when there's a beautiful woman at your table!"

Todd sat back down in his chair laughing.

"You're a lunatic!"

"You're right," answered Todd, "But I'm harmless, and I really don't care what you do. Okay?"

The harshness in Laura's face melted.

Todd filled their mugs with beer, then held his up in the air, "Here's to squid pizza and Chicago blues."

She picked up her mug. "To squid pizza and Chicago blues."

As they drank and chatted, Tony reappeared from the kitchen carrying their pizza. He stopped in front of them and kissed the tips of his fingers. "The work of art is ready!" he exclaimed, placing the steaming pizza on a cork pad and serving their plates.

Todd and Laura dug into their meal. Their conversation was lively and fuelled their appetites. Within half an hour the pizza had disappeared. Todd glanced at his watch, "We better get a move on if we want to catch some blues tonight."

Laura nodded.

After paying for the meal, Todd took a ten-dollar bill from his wallet and placed it in a well-worn cookie jar next to the cash register.

Laura looked at the label on the cookie jar. "Sean's Club?" she asked.

"It's something Tony does," was Todd's reply.

CHAPTER 3

The emergency room buzzed with activity with orderlies scurrying about like ants and stretchers flashing into examining rooms. Others were being wheeled onto elevators on the way to surgery. A few sat motionless in dark recesses, their occupants silenced by white sheets drawn loosely over them.

"Dr. Mendoza please report to ER. Dr. Mendoza please report to ER."

Stephanie Mendoza looked up at the hospital intercom speaker. "Typical night," she thought. "I'm here fifteen minutes early and ER is already swamped." She did up the last couple of buttons on her lab coat, clipped on her ID badge and headed down the hall towards emergency.

A stretcher wheeled past her with a doctor running along side, his hands pressing a blood stained dressing against a gaping chest wound. "Thank God you're in early Stef! The loonies are out early tonight!"

Mendoza watched her colleague disappear down the corridor. She snapped on a pair of examination gloves as she entered the ER department.

Stephanie checked in at the main desk, "Mendoza in! Mendoza in!"

A nurse grabbed a clipboard and turned towards Stephanie. "It's a wild one Stef!" she said.

"What do we have Kathy?" Mendoza asked.

"Three hot ones; gunshot in twelve, possible OD in four, beating victim in six," replied the nurse.

"Triage?"

"Do four, twelve, then six."

Stephanie motioned to a nearby nurse, "Well Frank, it looks like we're on together again tonight. We'd better get to number four."

Mendoza did her initial assessment with cool profession-alism. "Pin point pupils, needle tracks, and shallow breathing.

Looks like an overdose. Regular shooter. This could be a tough one. Frank, give me vitals."

"Resps just 8. Pulse 120. BP 100/60," replied Frank.

"Give me an 8.5 tube. Frank, have you got an IV in?"

"IV in."

Stephanie worked frantically trying to keep the patient breathing. Her face was like granite as she barked out commands while getting a breathing tube and ventilator in position. "Tube's in. Get a portable chest. Vent at 12 minute assist. Now let's start Narcan. Point 4 every 2 minutes until he wakes up. Watch for seizures folks as we have a regular user here. Better have some Ativan ready."

Frank responded with the data, "Resps now 12. Pulse down to 100."

"That's better. He's coming around. Let's keep at it people. Start gastric lavage," Mendoza directed. Within ten minutes relief flashed across her face. "Okay. It looks like he's stabilized. Call Dr. Osterman and tell him this one is on the way. She looked at the nurse and gave him a wink, "Great work, Frank. Let's go to number twelve."

After quickly checking the shooting victim's vital signs, Stephanie listened to the patient's chest and felt his trachea to make sure there were no breathing obstructions. Mendoza examined the wound, commenting to the nurse as she went, "Looks like a small caliber bullet. Upper right quadrant just above the collarbone. No exit point. Bullet's probably hit the shoulder blade and fragmented."

She looked down at the terrified face on the stretcher. "Can you move the fingers in your right hand?"

The man's eyes bulged with fear.

She asked again, "Can you move the fingers in your right hand?"

The man moaned, "No, no I can't. I can't feel anything in my arm."

"Possible nerve damage," she thought as she turned to an

orderly. "See if Thompson's available and get this one to X-ray and book surgery right away." Mendoza looked around for an orderly.

"Frank, there's no one free. Can you take this patient into pre-op right away?"

"Sure Stef. Be back in a minute," replied Frank as he pushed the stretcher down the hall.

"On to six," Stephanie thought as she picked her way through the melee of stretchers. As she entered the examination station she grabbed the chart that hung from the foot of the patient's bed. One of the nurses in ER had already entered the patient's vital signs.

She felt a hand on her shoulder. It was the attending nurse. "As beatings go this one's not too bad. A few lacerations on her face. Possible fractured ribs, fourth, maybe fifth on the right side. Heavy bruising and some swelling, could be some risk of a pneumo. Check thetachycardia. We may be looking at a coke baby who's party has gone bad."

Stephanie took a quick look at how the patient was dressed, noting her upscale attire, "Designer labels. Definitely not off the street. Doesn't look like a regular hitter to me. Probably a recreational user," she said, "Better get some expiration chest X-rays done to verify whether or not we're dealing with a pneumothorax." As she scrawled some instructions on the chart her eyes caught the name of the patient, freezing her pen on the chart. She moved to the head of the stretcher and looked down. "Oh my God! Laura!"

Snider looked up and tried to focus on the face staring down at her, managing a faint smile after a few moments, "That you Stef? Funny meeting you here."

Stephanie scanned the room and saw Frank re-entering. She raised her arm and waved, "Frank! Frank!"

His head snapped toward her. "Be right there Stef," said Frank as he dodged a couple of passing stretchers. "What's up?"

"Frank, after you get her IV's started, I need you to have an orderly get her into X-ray as soon as possible." She grabbed his arm. "She's a friend."

He saw the concern etched on her face. "Worried about a crash in X-ray?"

"Yes."

"I'll go with her."

"Thanks."

"Don't worry Stef. I'll let the folks in the lab know you have a special interest in this one. They'll put a rush on the film. I'll let you know where your friend is after X-ray is done with her."

"Okay." Stephanie watched silently as Frank pushed Laura's stretcher down the hall.

"Dr. Mendoza we need you over here!"

Stephanie looked up to see a nurse waving frantically toward an ambulance driver wheeling in another patient. The patient coughed, splattering blood across the floor. Mendoza moved toward the stretcher, raising her arm and yelling out toward the duty station, "Kathy! Kathy!"

"Yeah!"

"Page the trauma team!"

"Already on it!"

Mendoza reached the stretcher in an instant, looking expectantly at the ambulance driver.

"Three car pile up on the Inter-State. Almost lost this guy twice coming over."

She checked for a pulse. "Tachy and thready." Stephanie turned to the main desk and raised her arm, "Kathy, I need an open trauma room! Now!"

The duty nurse scanned her computer screen, "Okay...room four is open."

Stephanie ran down the hall along side the stretcher as they moved the patient into the room. The trauma team quickly assembled around the patient. They tried IV lines and bags, blood transfusions, tubes in the chest. Finally Mendoza called for defibrillation. The paddles crackled a half dozen times. Each sent a violent shock surging through the limp body on the table in front of her. Finally Mendoza stood upright, eyes closed. She took a deep breath and turned to one of the trauma team nurses. "Lost him. Is the family here?"

"I'm not sure."

Stephanie looked down at her blood-smeared gloves and gown. "Please find out about the family as quickly as you can. I better get cleaned up. This news will be bad enough for the family without me looking this way. I'll be back in a few minutes," Mendoza said as she exited the trauma room.

Stephanie snapped off her gloves and put them into the biohazard disposal receptacle, and removed her stained operating gown. Witnessing a life pass through her hands never got any easier. After Mendoza finished cleaning up she returned to ER. The supervisor of the X-ray department greeted her as soon as she entered.

"I need to show you something," said the supervisor as she led Stephanie down the hall to the X-ray examination room. "You can see this shoulder is in bad shape. Looks like the bullet shattered here. There's a good chance that the bullet got a nerve going in. Based on how it fragmented once it hit this bone, there's a good chance it nicked an artery. There's lots of swelling in the area. I looked at the patient before I came down. His shoulder is bruising up quickly. Looks like we could have plenty of internal bleeding. If we don't get in there to assess the damage and fix it quickly he may not make it. Surgery tells me that Thompson's tied up for at least another two hours. That's why I came down with the film to show you personally. Can you take this one?"

"What room?"

"Op three."

"Okay. Let Kathy know. I'll be there in a couple of minutes. I'll go scrub up."

The shoulder operation took almost two hours. Stephanie was able to close the damaged artery and after suturing the incision she washed, changed once again, and returned to the emergency room.

Frank spotted her as she entered, running over immediately. "Your friend Snider is going to be okay. Dr. Urbitz assessed her. One cracked rib, no pneumo."

"Thank God," Stephanie replied.

"He gave her a pain-killer and booked her into a ward room for overnight observation. Everything looks pretty good. She should be released in the morning."

"What room is she in?"

"2510."

"I'll check in on her once things quiet down a little."

"Stef."

"Yeah."

"She'll still be a looker. Plastics did a nice job suturing her facial lacerations," Frank said with a wink.

Mendoza smiled, "Thanks a million, Frank."

"No problem," he replied as he scanned the room. "We'd better move on to our next patient."

✳

Four hours later the caseload cleared enough for Mendoza to take her first shift break. She went to check on Laura. On the way to Snider's room Stephanie's mind was racing. She remembered the fifth grade when Laura first arrived in California. How they hit it off right away and became best friends. High school. Graduation. Sailing. The beach. Mutual friends. And finally how they went off to different colleges and gradually drifted apart. A voice inside Stephanie told her that finding Laura in the emergency room during her shift was more than just a coincidence. It also told her that she needed to help an old friend.

CHAPTER 4

As Laura awoke she tried shifting her weight onto her left side and was jolted by a sharp pain.

"You'll have to take it very easy for a couple of days."

Laura peaked over her right shoulder and saw Stephanie Mendoza seated in the chair next to her bed.

"How long have you been here?"

"About half an hour. I stopped in at four-thirty but you were still out like a light. I figured you'd come around after my shift ended."

"What time is it?"

"Almost eight-thirty."

"AM or PM?"

Stephanie chuckled, "AM. Do you have to ask that very often?"

"Depends."

"Like the morning after a beach party?"

"Oh, I don't want to remember those." Laura chuckled, holding her side. "Ouch!"

"It's good to see you again Laura. It's probably been at least five years."

"Good to see you too, Stef. When did you move to Chicago?"

"Nearly three years ago after I graduated from med school." She put her hand on Laura's shoulder, "Hey, there's no reason to stay cooped up in here. Let's get you checked out so we can make some time to catch up. When's your flight home?"

Snider looked surprised, "How do you know I need a flight?"

"The hospital responded to an emergency call about you from the hotel. While the ambulance was bringing you over our folks in admissions spoke to the security manager who checked your hotel registration information for us. Since your home address was shown as a suburb of Los Angeles and your hotel reservation was made through an L.A. travel agent it was pretty obvious you were from out of town. I didn't figure you'd drive all the way from L.A. to Chicago in the winter."

"Yeah, yeah. What you really wanted to know was if I had medical coverage," replied Laura with an impish grin.

Mendoza smiled, "Ah, I see you know the routine. Well, under normal circumstances that would have been a consideration." She paused, "Although it appears you don't have to worry about your visit with us since the hotel has asked us to charge them instead. That's unusual."

"Maybe unusual but not unexpected for a special customer." Laura looked for a reaction from Mendoza. None came. "Anyway, you're right. I've got a full fare ticket back to L.A. but I'm not locked into a specific return date."

A broad smile broke over Stephanie's face, "That's great! Why don't you check out of the hotel and bunk in with me? My condo's small, but it does have two bedrooms. We could spend a few days catching up. And, I'll be around to make sure those ribs of yours are okay."

Laura reached her hand across her chest and held Stephanie's, "Thanks Stef. I'd really like that. It's been too long."

"Good. Let's get you up and out of here."

After Laura was released from the hospital Stephanie drove her to the hotel and offered to help her pack up her belongings.

"No, I can handle packing up my things," said Laura as she declined the offer. "Why don't you grab something in the coffee shop? When I'm packed up I'll call for a bellman to carry my bags down."

"Okay, if that's what you want," Stephanie replied pensively then motioned to the coffee shop, "I'll wait for you in there."

"Thanks Stef." Snider turned and entered a waiting elevator.

A half an hour later she reappeared in the coffee shop. "Well, I'm all yours. Just like the song. My bags are packed and I'm ready to go."

As Stephanie drove across town to her condominium the two women reminisced about their time together in California. The old bonds between them were rekindled.

"Remember in the fifth grade when we swore we'd be life-long friends?" Stephanie asked.

"It was at the beach, I don't remember the oath but I remember the penalty!" said Laura.

The two women feigned a shudder, "Kiss a toad on the lips!" The laugh hurt Laura's ribs.

"I remember the oath," said Stephanie.

"Come on, you don't!"

"No, really. I do."

"Okay let's hear it," Laura challenged.

Stephanie put her right hand over her heart as she spoke, "Magic ocean, magic sky, here's the promises I make says I. I promise to always be your friend. I promise to always tell you the truth. I promise to always help you when you need it. I promise to always keep any secrets you tell me. If I ever break any of these promises I will kiss a toad on the lips."

Laura's eyes widened as she slapped the palms of her hands on her lap several times, "That's it! That's it! Now I remember it too! How did you remember?"

"I don't know. Fear of toads left me scarred for life I suppose." Stephanie pointed to the right. "See that red brick building next to the tall, gray one? That's home. Tell you what, I'll pull up in front and we'll put your bags in the lobby. Then, I'll park the car in the underground garage and come up to meet you. After you get settled in we can chat over a cup of coffee just like when we were in high school."

She stopped her car at the lobby entrance and placed Snider's bags inside next to the elevator. "I'll be a couple of minutes." She shook her index finger at Laura, "And don't even think about being a martyr by trying to lift any of these. Your ribs need complete rest for a few days. I'll go park the car and meet you back up here in the lobby."

"Yes, mommy," Laura replied as she rolled her eyes.

"You're still impossible."

"I do my best."

"See you in a minute," Stephanie replied as she went outside to move her car.

Laura stood patiently in the lobby waiting for Mendoza to reappear. "I wonder how this is going to go?" she thought. "It's been a long time." Snider smiled as she remembered some of the things the two of them did together in high school. "Those were special times. It will be good to spend some time together." She heard the elevator bell ring and turned to see Mendoza exiting the elevator.

"Well you can see that I don't live in a palace, but it is nice and cozy. Let's get your things upstairs." Stephanie picked up Laura's bags and moved them over to the elevator. "Home is on the third floor." Once inside the apartment, Stephanie moved Laura's bags into the guest bedroom. "While you unpack, I'll brew a pot of coffee. Still take it with double cream and sugar?"

"Yeah, I'm still a wimp."

Stephanie went into the kitchen to prepare the coffee.

In a few minutes Laura appeared in the kitchen. "Mmm, smells fantastic! Let's sit at the kitchen table, just like the old days." The colours on the placemats blazed in the sunlight that streamed in through the window. The women sat across from each other.

"So, how have you been, Laura?"

She motioned to her rib cage. "Up until yesterday things were going great. I don't think Chicago agrees with me," she said forcing a nervous chuckle.

Stephanie sipped her coffee and studied Laura for a few moments. "One of my best friends in Chicago is a science teacher."

Laura looked puzzled, "That's interesting."

"My friend can get us a toad if you need one."

Laura's expression hardened. "What's that supposed to

mean?" She got up from her chair and walked over to the sliding balcony doors, standing motionless, staring off into the distance.

"Come on Laura. Tell me what's going on. It's not everyday a person gets to treat their best friend from high school in a hospital emergency room." Stephanie waited for a reply. When none came she continued, "How long have you been using cocaine?"

Snider's head snapped towards Stephanie. "I don't know what you're talking about."

Stephanie's voice was calm and measured, "Laura, I work in the emergency department of a large Chicago hospital. I've seen this thousands of times over the past three years." Her eyes pleaded for a response.

Snider turned her gaze back to the balcony door. "It's no big deal. Started after college."

"How often do you use it? Everyday?"

"A few times a month when I feel like it."

"You're playing with fire Laura. It's expensive and…"

Laura cut off Stephanie's comment. "Look, I do it because I like how it makes me feel. I make a lot of money Stef. I can afford to buy whatever I want. My clothes have all got designer labels. I wear 14 carat, not cheap costume jewelry. I drive a Mercedes, not a old beater like some people I know." Her gaze returned to Stephanie, "I get whatever I want."

Stephanie looked at her friend. Then glanced down at the kitchen table. "Your coffee is getting cold. You always hated cold coffee."

Laura's eyes flicked down at her coffee cup, "Yeah, I do hate cold coffee. It makes me gag." Her gaze returned to the window.

Mendoza could see Laura's jaw muscles flexing. "Medical school was a real grind. God, we must have put in a hundred hours a week between classes, assignments, research and ward work. It's a miracle any of us survived. The experience made a lot of us pretty close. Sometimes too close. I followed a fellow intern out here to Chicago to do our residencies. It didn't work out. He defined relationships in a much broader context and a little differently than I did."

"Sorry to hear that, Stef. Anyone in your life now?"

"Just work for now. Still hurts a bit."

Laura returned to the kitchen table, "Sorry I snapped at you Stef. It really is good to see you again. Sometimes it's easy to forget who your real friends are."

"When did you get into town?"

"Thursday last week."

"Business?"

"More of a working holiday."

Stephanie let the reply pass without further comment. "Want your coffee warmed up?"

Laura smiled, "No, let's dump this cup and start fresh. I feel like polishing off this pot off and making another one after that. We haven't had a 'two pots of coffee' talk for years."

Stephanie poured the contents of Laura's cup down the sink and refilled it, then added some cream and sugar. "How did you end up in emergency last night?" she asked as she handed Snider the fresh cup of coffee.

"I met a friend of a friend in the bar at the hotel. We went upstairs for a little fun. Did a few lines of coke. I guess the coke hit him bad and he turned on me and started playing pretty rough. I remember yelling at him to stop. The next thing I recall hotel security was banging on the door. He wouldn't stop hitting me so the guards used their passkeys to get in. I felt pretty groggy, but I remember them pulling him off me and getting him out of the room in a hurry. I guess that's when I passed out. The next thing I remember I was getting wheeled into the hospital."

"You know who this guy was?"

"Sure. Like I said, he was the friend of a friend."

"Are you going to press charges?"

"No. It's already settled." replied Laura, seeing the puzzled look on Stephanie's face. "When I went to check out of my suite in the hotel this morning my bill was already paid in full."

27

"A suite in that hotel? That must have run close to seven hundred dollars a night."

"Six-sixty plus taxes to be exact. Ten days with meals, laundry, some incidentals and taxes brought the total up to nearly seventy-three hundred."

"Your friend of a friend paid?"

"I'm not sure. Could have been him or it could have been the hotel."

"Why would the hotel write it off?"

"Goodwill."

Mendoza looked puzzled.

"My friend of a friend is the CEO of a large multi-national corporation and a regular client of the hotel," Laura continued. "His company also uses the property for a large number of their meetings and conventions. The last thing the hotel or my friend need is bad publicity. It was easier just to cover my account. My friend of a friend left me a little something for my trouble."

"What was that?"

"An envelope with three thousand cash in it." Laura watched Stephanie's reaction then continued, "That's twice my usual fee for an executive meeting."

"I see."

"What's the matter? Did I shock you?"

"Is your life what you want, Laura?"

"I've got a condo in an exclusive area of L.A. Designer clothes. A Mercedes. A stock portfolio like a doctor's. I've got everything I want."

"I didn't ask what you had Laura. I asked if your life is what you want it to be."

"That's a stupid question. Life comes with a price tag. Everyone sells themselves out for something. At least I know what I want and I go out and get it."

"Is that why you do it?"

"You mean the money? I suppose that's a big part of it. But, there's also a feeling of power. When I see a certain look in their eyes I know I have them. They want me and they are willing to pay. The more I can make them pay, the more power I have. I did a guy on Tuesday night just for the fun of it. He was a small town type. From Wrightsville of all places. He actually expected he could get the works for a hundred. I got him up to three hundred and fifty before I took him upstairs. With some extras I made four and a quarter." After sipping her coffee Laura chuckled, "He probably thought he had died and gone to heaven with what I did for him. I guess he'll never know he was a charity case."

"How did you get started?"

"After college I really got into partying. In L.A. it's easy to meet young studs with lots of money. One day it dawned on me that there was no need to give it away. So I started selling it. I found that if I was discreet I could develop a very select clientele and I didn't have to work too hard. I figured out I could make a lot of money and have fun doing it."

"Fun?"

"Why not. It still feels great whether you're getting paid for it or not. I suppose that's why my clients are willing to pay me what they do. I love doing it and it shows."

"I can't even pretend to understand that Laura."

"No one is asking you to."

Stephanie glanced at her watch. "Look, it's almost eleven and I've been up for over twenty-six hours. If I don't crash and get five or six hours sleep I'm going to be a basket case. I was planning to go out tonight and see a speaker I've heard some fantastic things about, do you want to come?"

"I don't know, maybe. What's the topic?"

"Life."

CHAPTER 5

Let's go sleepyhead," said Laura as she shook her friend, "You slept through your alarm. If we're going to catch that speaker tonight you'd better get a move on!"

Stephanie's eyes snapped open, "What time is it?"

"Almost six o'clock."

Stephanie fumbled out of bed. "Okay, I'll have a quick shower. We'll grab something to eat on the way."

By six forty-five they had picked up some hamburgers, fries, and drinks at a drive-through restaurant and were on their way to the convention centre.

"What made you decide to come tonight, Laura?"

"Curiosity as much as anything else. What's this guy's name anyway?"

"Robert Parnell."

"Can't say that I've heard of him. Is he one of those motivational types?"

"I suppose some people refer to him that way."

"So what makes him different than the other self-help speakers out there? I've always thought they were all a bunch of Fast Buck Charlies."

"I've never seen him before so I don't know first hand. Other people have told me that his material really made them think. He talks about human potential and how we can find our place in the world. How we can make a difference. He's supposed to be an incredibly powerful speaker."

After parking the car, the two women entered the facility and found a pair of seats about twenty rows from the stage. Within twenty minutes the lights dimmed and an off-stage announcer introduced Robert Parnell.

As he made his entrance, two cameramen with shoulder-mounted video cameras broadcast his image on a video wall that was positioned in the middle of the stage. The audience applauded his appearance.

As Parnell took centre stage he looked out toward the blackness that enveloped the audience. "Can we have the house lights on please?" he asked in a calm tone. Within a few seconds banks of lights began flicking on throughout the hall. He smiled noticeably as the audience came into view, and he began speaking to them.

"I'd like to thank each of you for taking time out of your busy lives to come and visit with me tonight. I know it can be difficult with all of the other commitments you no doubt have. I'll try my best to make sure your time was well spent being here tonight."

Robert strolled across the stage and stopped at the edge, looking directly at a man sitting in the fourth row. "I've often heard myself described as a motivational speaker. Now, I'm not sure what picture that creates in your mind. But, for me, when I think of a motivational speaker, I get a picture of some late night TV show."

As he spoke Robert wandered toward a prop table on the stage. "I always think of one of those infomercials that I end up watching at three in the morning when I can't sleep. There's usually someone dressed in an impeccable suit and every hair on his head is perfectly groomed, and he's always trying to sell me something."

The audience began to stir.

He casually picked up an audiocassette box from the table on the stage. "You've probably even heard something like this." Robert held the box in front of his shoulder and began to talk using a strong Southern drawl, speaking rapidly and sharply. "My friends, do you want to change your life? Do you want to be more successful than you ever dreamed possible? Do you want to make more money in one year than you'd otherwise make in a lifetime? Do you want to be more popular? Do you want to have such a steamy sex life that People Magazine will dedicate an entire issue to you?"

Parnell's voice dropped in tone and slowed. "Well, for only

three easy payments of thirty-nine ninety-five, you too can own Dr. P's Magic Motivational Tapes! These tapes are guaranteed, I say guaranteed, to change your life! And, if you act now, you will receive, absolutely free, Dr. P's voice enhancement training audiotapes. You will learn proper enunciation, pronunciation, projection, and other techniques known only to professional speakers! Imagine. You can learn to talk just like Dr. P! And, make radio commercials anywhere in Mississippi!"

The audience roared with laughter.

Parnell stopped and scanned the crowd waiting for the hall to settle. He then spoke slowly in his natural voice. "Well, I hate to disappoint some of you. But, that's not what I do. What we will do tonight is share some thoughts on how we might be able to change our lives, even if it's just by a little bit. I think that's what all of us want. Just to be able to make our lives a little bit better, one day at a time. So let's relax and have some fun."

He moved to the edge of the stage, then climbed down onto the floor of the hall and began speaking as he walked up one of the aisles. The two cameramen scrambled down from the stage after him. For over two hours Robert's sincerity and passion for his beliefs held the crowd in total control. During his presentation he often sat down next to members of the audience, talking to them one-on-one. At other times he got so engrossed in his topic that he ran up the aisle-ways almost screaming at the top of his lungs. His compassion for people flowed freely. He could feel their pain, their joy, and their frustrations. He gave them the best he had to offer; his energy, dreams of the future, and visions of a better world. Throughout it all the two cameramen scurried about so they could catch his image and project it through the video wall.

Finally, Robert returned to the stage and picked up a show card from the table, holding it up to the audience. It was a diagram showing three concentric circles. The outermost circle was marked 'Badge'. The first interior circle was marked 'Body'. The smallest circle was marked 'Being'.

"If each of you could walk away tonight with only a few things you could remember, I hope this diagram would be one of them." The hall was totally silent as he spoke, the image of the diagram filling the video wall.

"Virtually all of the stress and turmoil in the world is directly related to what you see on the monitors in front of you. These circles represent the three possible ways you and I can relate to each other, as well as the ways we can define ourselves, and those around us."

"The outer circle is the badge we wear. That's when we pigeon hole ourselves or other people based on what we do: vice-president, professor, homosexual, husband, wife, doctor, drug addict, thief, engineer, teacher, prostitute. We even put labels on people because of some religious orientation. He's a Jew. She's a Catholic. He's a Muslim. She's a Baptist."

"We relate to people based on these meaningless labels. We judge people as good or bad, based on what they do. We confuse the person with the activity. We equate their worth as human beings with the words we use to describe them."

Robert motioned to the diagram. "The next circle represents our body, the package we find ourselves in. Think about how often we pass judgment on someone based on the colour of their skin, the slant of their eyes, their height, their weight, the size of their breasts, the length of their penis. We use all kinds of arbitrary physical factors to judge people. To decide whether they are worthy of our attention, our friendship. Whether we should hire them to do a job. If we want them to be one of our neighbours. And in some parts of the world, whether they should be allowed to live."

"Throughout the history of human existence countless millions of people have died because of these first two circles. Every time we judge another person as unworthy because of one of these labels we put on them we take our society one step further down the road of destruction."

"Look at what we have done as a species. We have gone to

war. Raped. Murdered. Tortured. Obliterated complete cities. Committed genocide. Just think of some of the places around the world and the scenes of horror television has delivered to us. Bosnia. Rwanda. Kosovo. The inhumanity and senselessness of the suicide attacks on the World Trade Center and the Pentagon."

"We only have to watch the evening news to see the carnage that happens everyday in our own communities. All because of an arbitrary label placed on one human being by another. When we label others we make them something less than human and an easy target for our personal frustrations and insecurities."

"Do you realize that in over two-thousand years of recorded human history less than fifteen of them have been spent with no documented war happening somewhere on this planet?"

Robert paused as he was visibly shaken. After regaining his composure he continued with his voice firm and measured. "The destructive power now in the hands of human beings is exponential. We cannot afford war. We cannot afford to rape and murder and torture. We cannot afford genocide. We cannot afford the faceless brutality of terrorism. If we do not change our path our species will cease to exist. The roots of our depravity, as a species and as individuals, are anchored in the labels we put on each other. Without labels there is no convenient justification for our brutality. The mayhem we create. Without labels there is no separateness in the human experience."

Robert made a wide sweeping gesture toward the audience. He then pointed to the interior circle on the diagram. The one marked 'Being'. "This is what we all are! Ninety-nine percent of what we are is not our badge, and it is not our body. What we really are is invisible to us. We are energy. We are life energy. We are thought energy. Each of us has the capacity to change the world by how we use our thoughts. By how we use our life energy. By the choices we make."

Robert paused then asked the members of the audience a question. "Raise your hand if you think that you will accomplish enough in your life that your obituary will run in one of the country's leading business publications."

He looked out into the audience and saw that virtually no one raised a hand. "I want to tell you about a newspaper article I read. It was about a man whose obituary did run in one of the country's leading business papers. The article was full of interviews with people who had nothing but kind things to say about this man. They commented on how he had impacted their lives in a positive way, and how he made a difference."

Robert collected his thoughts and brought his hands together, as if in prayer, the tips of his middle fingers pressing against his lips. He took a deep breath and began to speak, extending his arms out to the audience. "This man who touched so many people wasn't a high powered business leader. He wasn't an artist, or a scientist, or a teacher. On the surface this man was just another vagrant. Someone who lived on the streets in the same neighbourhood for decades. In the summer he slept on a park bench or in the subway if it was raining, on exhaust grates in the winter. Just one person out of the multitude of homeless people in cities across North America today."

"Yet, this man changed the lives of those around him. People commented how he was always there to help them. How he cared for the neighbourhood children, even buying them candy if he happened on a little bit of money. He was always there to share a joke or funny story when others were down, and gave guidance to countless confused teenagers, getting many of them off the streets. The same streets where he chose to live for more than thirty years."

Robert reached into the pocket of his suit jacket and unfolded a newspaper clipping and held it motionless so one of the cameramen could focus in on it. "He was hit by a car and died a few days later in the hospital. The people of the inner city community where he lived took up a collection to pay for an obituary in this national business paper. They wanted people all across the country to know how important this man was to their community. And, how much their lives had been touched by him. They even turned the park bench where he used to sleep on summer evenings into a shrine."

He folded up the newspaper clipping and put it back in his pocket. "This man teaches us all lessons about personal values and service to others. He teaches us that everyone has the capacity to make a difference to the world."

"This man never achieved material success. His body was small and frail, beaten with time. Most of us would have labeled him a bum, a vagrant, or worse. Some of us would have crossed to the other side of the street to avoid him when he was pan-handling for pocket change. Most of us would have simply passed him by without saying a word. But this man was a success. He was a success because he chose to make the world around him a more compassionate and caring place."

The audience sat silent, all eyes riveted on Parnell. "Those of you who have lived in Chicago for a while may be aware of some of the special people in your city. People who are doing extraordinary things in the service of others. People like Tony Ambruzzo who has dedicated twenty-five years of his life to Sean's Club; a youth drop in centre he created. He's helped thousands of teenagers get on track. He's encouraged them to continue with their education. Nearly eight hundred are now college graduates. A few have gone on to earn Ph.D.'s. And Tony continues on. For him, every day of life is a celebration. A labor of love."

"Before I leave you tonight, I'd like to give you a picture to remember in your minds. That picture is of a small, skinny, six-year-old kid. I guess in today's lingo you'd say he looked like a nerd; big ears, glasses, crew cut."

A few chuckles rose from the audience.

"I want you to picture him in a school yard being sur-rounded by a group of bigger, tougher kids who are picking on him, taunting him. Now, try and feel what that kid felt. Too small to fight back, and because his stuttering was so bad he couldn't even defend himself verbally. I want you to picture that little six-year-old boy walking home, his nose is bloody, the wind is drying the tears on his cheeks."

Parnell spoke slowly, with great emotion. "Picture that same skinny kid, glasses, crew cut, starting to grow up and going all the way through grade school. Every day is the same, the taunting, and the name-calling. Then, he goes to high school and takes his speech impediment with him. He meets the same ridicule from his classmates through all those years. After high school he starts working in a warehouse on the night shift. He works hard and he gets promoted and he's more terrified than he's ever been in his entire life. Why? He's in customer service and it's his first day on the job. It's eight o'clock in the morning, he's in early and he's staring at the telephone on his desk. Knowing that it's going to ring and he's terrified. Terrified because he can't even say the name of the company that employs him."

Robert studied people in the audience. They were all sitting in stone silence. "That small, skinny, six-year-old kid, big ears, glasses, crew cut, would like to thank each and every one of you for coming out tonight to hear him speak this evening. And for those of you who are not completely happy with your life, he'd like you to take three thoughts home with you tonight."

"Change your thoughts and you will change yourself. Change yourself and you will change your life. Change your life and you will help change the world. Thank you."

As Robert left the stage the audience rose to its feet and gave him a standing ovation. Many were crying. An announcement came over the public address system. "Ladies and gentlemen this brings the presentation portion of our program to a close. We have set up a table at the foot of the stage where Robert Parnell will be available for autographs. Thank you for coming tonight, and please have a safe journey home."

As Stephanie turned to leave the hall, Laura grabbed her arm. "Stef, I have to go and talk to Robert Parnell."

Stephanie glanced at her watch, "It's after ten o'clock and it will take us almost an hour to get home." She looked toward the stage, "Laura, there's a huge line up forming. We don't have time."

"I have to talk to him."

"Why?"

"Because I met Tony Ambruzzo on Tuesday night."

Before she could say another word, Laura headed off toward the stage. Stephanie had no choice but to follow her. There was a small book display off to the left of the autograph table. Laura purchased one of Parnell's books. She then took her place in the autograph line. After waiting for nearly thirty minutes, she was finally face to face with Parnell. She handed him her book.

"I had to meet you in person Mr. Parnell."

He looked up puzzled. "Why is that?"

"I met Tony Ambruzzo on Tuesday last week."

A wide smile erupted over Parnell's face. "Then you are a lucky lady indeed! Tony is a very special person. Where did you meet him?"

"I had dinner at his restaurant."

"Really? How did you find it? Not many people know about it."

"I went on sort of a blind date with a bartender I met."

Parnell nodded and smiled, "I understand. How would you like me to address this autograph?"

"To Laura Snider."

Robert penned a personal note to Laura, handed her back the book, then asked, "And would that bartender's name be Todd O'Brien?"

Laura's jaw dropped, "How would you know his name?"

"He hired me to come and speak here tonight."

CHAPTER 6

After Laura got Parnell's autograph she and Stephanie left the convention centre to drive back to the condominium. The ride was uncomfortably quiet with Stephanie trying to start a conversation several times but finding her friend distant and preoccupied.

Stephanie glanced at Laura, noticing a tear running down her cheek.

"Are you okay?"

Laura brushed away the tear, "Can we go out for dinner tomorrow night? It'll be kind of a farewell celebration. I've decided to fly back to L.A. on Monday morning."

"Sure. Dinner out sounds like a good idea. What did you have in mind?"

"I don't know, nothing fancy. How about going out for pizza?"

"Pizza it is."

As they continued on the drive back to Stephanie's condominium Laura grew silent again, her tears flowing more freely. After a few moments she regained her composure and started to speak, "Thanks for taking me to the convention centre tonight, Stef. I needed to hear what Robert Parnell had to say."

"I'm glad you found his message useful."

Laura's eyes were staring straight ahead as she spoke, "There was one part where I felt he was speaking just to me. Do you remember when he was talking about making choices, that our lives are a result of the choices we make?"

"Uh-huh."

"He asked us to accept the idea that we had the power to choose our parents."

"I remember that."

"Then he asked us to also accept that, prior to us making our selection, we had the ability to look into the future and see exactly what was going to happen as a result of the choice we were about to make." As Laura continued she was still staring off into the distance. "He said that if we could accept responsibility for the outcome of our choice of parents, we would never be a slave to the past. We would never have to live with hate or blame directed towards our parents, because we knew what they were going to do when we picked them. He said that we would be able to look at them in a new light. Rather than blame and hate the things they did we would be able to focus on what we were supposed to learn from the experience, and how the experience helped us grow."

"It certainly is a very different perspective of life and choices."

"Stef, when he was saying those things I was thinking about my parents. My dad. I tried to picture myself choosing my parents. It's a hard thing to imagine."

"I found it difficult too, Laura. It's a concept that most people would find hard to accept."

"I'd like to believe him. I'd like to believe I knew what was going to happen. I'd like to believe that everything happened because there was a lesson to learn. I'd like to believe there was a bigger purpose behind it all. I'd like to believe there was an answer."

She started to drift off again.

Stephanie pulled into a shopping centre parking lot and stopped her car. "Laura, what can I do to help you? I've never seen you like this before."

"I guess I haven't thought about my past quite like this before. It's... hard."

"What's hard?"

"To forgive."

"Who?"

"My dad."

"Forgive your dad? For what?"

Laura took a deep breath, drew her lips in and tilted her head back slowly, staring at the pattern in the headliner of

Stephanie's car, tears trickling down her cheeks. "For taking away my childhood."

Mendoza gasped, "Oh God! Laura, I never knew."

"Nobody knew. When a daughter promises her dad she won't tell, she doesn't tell."

Stephanie reached over and held her in her arms, Laura weeping openly. "Do you want to talk about it?"

"I…don't know."

Stephanie held her friend as her mind flashed back to their lives in California. The fifth grade. She remembered meeting Laura. Her braids. How shy she was. How the other children in the class avoided her for the first couple of weeks.

"Did it happen before you moved to California?"

"Yes."

"How old were you?"

"Six, when it first happened."

"So, it happened more than once?"

"It happened…too many times."

Stephanie rocked gently as she continued to hold Laura. "He's gone now, Laura. He's dead. He can't hurt you anymore. He can't do those things to you anymore."

"And he can never tell me he's sorry for what he did."

Stephanie bit her lower lip, "No, he can't."

Laura looked up at Stephanie, her eyes red with tears. "Why did he do it Stef? Why did he hurt me like he did? I was his daughter. How can a father hurt his daughter like that?"

"I don't know Laura. Maybe he never knew why either. Maybe he was too sick to know."

"Was he too sick to care? Was he too sick to feel shame when he left his daughter cowering in the corner? Was he too sick to notice my tears? Was he too sick to see my blood on the sheets?"

"He was…what he was. You can't change that now, Laura. He's dead. You're not. You're still here. You still have the rest of your life ahead."

"And it's a wonderful life to look forward to, isn't it? You as much said so yourself."

"Your life is what you want it to be."

Laura snapped, "No it's not! How can you say that? My life isn't what I wanted! My parents aren't what I wanted! Living in fear isn't what I wanted! Praying that my mom wouldn't go out for the evening isn't what I wanted! Hiding under the covers in shame isn't what I wanted!"

"What do you want the future to be?"

"I don't know! I just want the hurting to stop."

"Laura, you can stay with me as long as you want, as long as it takes you to make it through this. You're my friend." Stephanie reached over and lifted Snider's chin. "We made an oath together. Remember? I never break a promise. I'm never going to have to kiss a toad on the lips."

CHAPTER 7

There were so many people waiting in line for autographs after Robert's speech at the convention centre in Chicago that he was almost thirty-five minutes late leaving. Had it not been for a large tip to the taxi driver he would have missed his return flight home that evening. Parnell settled into his seat and picked up the in-flight magazine scanning the movie listings. Within a few seconds he returned it to the seat pocket in front of him having discovered that thirty-four airplane trips in fifteen days had exhausted his choices of reading material. As he tried to find a comfortable seating position he realized that the last couple of weeks, which had been an especially tough road trip, were finally coming to a close.

His gaze drifted out of the cabin window to the darkness surrounding the airplane. In the shadows he could see a beehive of activity: baggage handlers, signalmen, maintenance technicians. Robert became aware of someone standing next to him, placing a bag in the overhead bin. He looked up to see a huge, bear-like form with long brown hair and a thick, unruly beard. A smiling face came into view as the huge man overflowed in the seat next to him and extended his hand.

'Hi, I'm Bill Pearce. Glad to be sharing this flight with you.'

Parnell's hand disappeared in the other man's grasp as they shook hands. "Pleased to meet you Bill. I'm Robert Parnell."

Bill stared at Robert intently. "There's something familiar about you. Are you Robert Parnell the writer?"

"That's right. How did you know?"

"I'm a real book hound. I have a number of your books at home. I must have recognized you from one of the pictures on the jacket covers of your books. What takes you to L.A.?"

"A speaking engagement. And you?"

"Finally getting to go home for a while. I've been on the east coast for nearly four weeks straight doing video production work for clients. I can't wait to see my wife and kids."

"How many kids do you have?"

"Five. Four boys and a girl."

"Five! That must keep you hopping."

"My wife a lot more than me. How about you? Any kids?"

"No, my wife and I were not blessed in that way. You mentioned you've been gone for nearly four weeks. Even in my business I can't imagine being away from home that long, it must be really tough."

"Yeah, it's been brutal on everyone. I called home every night since I've been gone to talk to my kids, but nothing can take the place of actually being with them and holding them."

"I can only imagine what a special feeling that must be. You said you were doing some video production. What kind of business are you in, Bill?"

"I own a video production company. We do almost entirely corporate work. Product introductions. Training materials. That kind of stuff."

"How about rock videos? I hear that's a big part of the business, especially in L.A."

"We actually did a little bit of that a few years ago. Not my type of client though. They're tough to work with, and perhaps surprisingly, it's tough to get paid. We got burned a couple of times so we don't touch it any more."

"That's interesting. With all their money I wouldn't have thought that rock stars would be bad credit risks."

"Trust me on that one."

"So, you have to travel quite a bit?" Robert asked.

"Not as a rule. There's usually more than enough business in the L.A. area to keep us busy. One of my biggest clients wanted us to shoot an extensive piece that included all their facilities in the east as well as a series of major product introductions they held during the past three weekends for their dealers. That's why I couldn't get back sooner. I had to shoot each of the dealer events. How about you?"

"I can usually work my schedule so that my road trips only

last a maximum of five to seven days, although this one's been quite a bit longer than usual."

"Are you on your way home too?"

"No, this is my last stop before getting back."

"So, where do you call home?"

"Toronto."

"Home of the Blue Jays, Raptors, and Maple Leafs."

"You bet."

The two men continued chatting as the airplane taxied out to the runway, quickly becoming comfortable with each other and exchanging business cards by the time the airplane had reached cruising altitude.

"I have a question for you Robert."

"What's that Bill?"

"Well, over the past few years I've had a chance to read a number of your books and found that your writing covers some diverse topics. Some of the material you've done is obviously designed to help people improve their personal performance, and yet, other books you've written have got a spiritual message in them. What's the connection, or is there one?"

Parnell studied Pearce for a few seconds. "That's a fair question, Bill. I guess the only thing I've ever tried to do as a writer is help people along their journey of self discovery, regardless of where they may be along their path."

"Based on the fact that the comment you just made has a decidedly spiritual ring to it, I'd have to assume it's the spiritual side that is the most important to you. Given that, why would you write books that give people practical ways to improve their performance?"

"If someone's energy is totally consumed in dealing with the day-to-day struggles of life in a physical sense, there's no energy left for them to use on the spiritual side of their existence. Helping people unlock the doors to their personal performance so they can improve the physical world around them, frees up energy they can direct to their spiritual quest later on."

"So your ultimate goal as a writer is really the spiritual development of your readers?"

Parnell was growing increasingly comfortable with Pearce and sensed Bill's compassion and sincerity. "I don't see it as a this or that situation, but instead a this and that," Robert replied. "We all have physical and meta-physical components to our existence and since every life is unique, every journey of discovery for each life is unique. Ultimately what I'm trying to do is share my life experiences with other people with the hope that, by sharing it and trying to put it in some Universal context, it may help them with their journey."

Pearce thought for a moment. "That must be difficult. None of us can ever live someone else's life, or have the exact experiences that other people do. Even though we often say that we know how someone else feels, I think it's impossible for us to really know, because we have not lived that exact experience. All we can do is live our version of that experience. So, when we describe what we've done, or where we've been, or a Universal truth that we've discovered, it can never be fully understood by another person until they experience their version of it."

"I couldn't agree more with you Bill. It is very difficult. I guess I see us all as explorers marking a trail through the forest. We all are on our own particular journey, but we can be guided by the experiences of others."

"I like that analogy, Robert. I guess many of us are on spiritual journeys of one sort of another. What's your quest?"

"Now that question could take us into some interesting areas," Robert commented as he assessed Bill. "If I answer that you may end up thinking that I'm a lunatic."

Pearce sat back and looked at Parnell with disbelief. "I'm not sure how to take that last statement. You're a well- known author. I can't even imagine what you could say that would make me think that you're crazy."

"Bill, over the years I've had this kind of conversation with more than a few folks. They've all left the discussion scratching their heads and wondering when I'd be fitted for a straight-jacket."

Pearce looked Robert in the eye, "Okay. I can accept that. Give me the benefit of the doubt. I'm not like other people."

Parnell studied Pearce for a few moments then finally nodded his head. "Alright. Let's venture off into this discussion."

"Good," Bill replied. "So, what's your quest?"

"To find the root and meaning of our existence."

"Now there's something that is more than just a little challenging. If you can help the rest of us do that Robert, I'm all ears. Tell me where you've been with this."

Robert began his explanation in a somewhat reserved manner but soon his hand gestures became more animated as he continued to speak. "There's one thing that's at the root of our insecurity, and that's to learn why we're here. We all want to somehow discover, and know, that our being here isn't an accident. That we're not a cosmic mistake. That there is a higher purpose. If we don't have a sense of higher purpose we have no way of relating to the Universe or understanding our role in it, and we have an emptiness inside of us, a void. To try and fill it we tend to behave in bizarre ways as a means to try and create self-justification."

"Robert, how many of us know what our life purpose is? Some do, but how many Gandhi's can there be?"

"We can all make a difference to the world. Obviously we won't all affect it in the same way Gandhi did because how we choose to make that difference is unique for everyone. It all starts with how we define ourselves."

"In terms of what? Do you mean physically? Exoterically? Metaphysically?"

"All I can tell you is that, in my life, I discovered four ways I tried to define myself," replied Robert.

"Go on," encouraged Bill.

Parnell reached into his briefcase and took out a pen and a pad of paper. "Let me draw a small diagram to help illustrate these four struggles that I've experienced." He drew a five-inch by five-inch box and divided it into four equal quadrants. Then he used his pen to broaden the lines that separated the four quadrants and printed a heading over the square, 'The Search for Self'.

External Material	*Internal Material*
Internal Spiritual	*External Spiritual*

Robert marked the upper left hand quadrant 'external material' then continued his explanation. "I think most of us, not everyone but most of us, start off defining ourselves and our lives in material terms. We think that we are a success if we own a big house, a flashy car, that sort of thing. In fact, for many of us we are what we own, and we are what we do. Without these things we have no sense of self."

"You're talking to someone who lives in L.A. Material capital of the world."

"So, you're telling me I won't get an argument from you on this point?"

"Nope. I think it's very common for people to define themselves in strictly material terms. When you use the term 'external material' I assume you are referring to an external locus of control."

"Exactly."

"So by that you mean that people do not take responsibility for their own actions and performance. They blame external circumstances when they don't achieve the material success they want."

"Absolutely," Robert replied. "And, unless we move out of this external material state we never develop any further as human beings because we never take ownership for our lives. We end up stuck in a sea of self-pity, blaming the environment around us for everything. We can't even begin to think about defining ourselves in spiritual terms, since our physical needs have not been met."

"That sounds like classic Maslow theory. It may be true in the majority of cases, but wouldn't you agree that some people don't have a material orientation at all? Doesn't that give them a different starting point on this diagram?"

"Good point Bill. These four quadrants I've drawn out shouldn't be viewed as an absolute path that everyone follows in a particular order. I think many of us find ourselves in one of these states at one time or another in our lives. Perhaps some of us even bounce back and forth into some of these states numerous times throughout our lives. I know that I certainly have. Let me fill out the rest of this diagram." Parnell labeled the upper right quadrant 'internal material', the lower right 'external spiritual' and the lower left 'internal spiritual'. "As I mentioned earlier, I think we all want to learn what our purpose is in being here, and unless we discover our purpose, there is a hollowness, a void that we can't get rid of. If we can't come to grips with who we are and why we're here, how can we discover what it is we're supposed to do with our life?"

"There's no question that finding this understanding about one's purpose or life mission is critical. Victor Frankl's experiences in the Nazi concentration camps and his observations of the behaviors of inmates under those horrific conditions led him to his theories of logo-therapy," Bill added. "He discovered that a wide range of mental illnesses could be cured if the patient could discover their life purpose. Frankl was one of the pioneers in this area of psychoanalysis."

"Absolutely." Robert replied. He did some seminal work in this area. The challenge for most of us is that we don't take the therapy option to try to discover our life purpose, so in our minds we do the next best thing; we embark on a journey to define ourselves. I think in western culture that's normally done in material terms as we discussed earlier. Often we never get out of the 'external material' state because we spend our entire lives bitching and complaining to anyone who will listen. We moan about how we were taken advantage of. How someone else got all the breaks. How our boss or someone we worked with screwed us. How life owed us something and never paid up."

Bill nodded his head in agreement, "So many people end up looking for a saviour to give them the material things they think will give their lives meaning. They turn to the company, the government, the union, or some other organization, following them blindly, and waiting for someone or something to make them complete. In a way this search for material self-definition turns people into sheep chasing the latest fads and fashions, and makes them easy prey for the manipulators of the world."

"All because we don't have a sense of self, a sense of purpose," Robert said. "Some of us choose to leave this 'external material' state because we refuse to accept what we see in front of us. We want more out of life and we've learned that sitting on our rears and bitching about life hasn't gotten us anywhere. We get the rude awakening that there are no saviours. This is where self-help books and tapes serve a very useful purpose. They give us the inspiration and techniques to move out of the 'external material' state into the 'internal material' one. In this state, we still define ourselves in material terms and still wrap up our self-esteem in material possessions and job titles. But, at least we are actively participating in our existence and have taken the first big step in our journey by accepting some responsibility for our life."

"In that context I can see how your performance enhancement books fit in," said Bill. "So, let's suppose someone is in this 'internal material' state and they've achieved great success in a material sense. For many people there would be a temptation to stay in that state. After all, they're able to define themselves in very comfortable terms. They may also feel a sense of being in control of their lives."

"Many do," replied Robert.

Bill thought for a moment, "But your point is that the material success we've been chasing was just a surrogate for our real goal, which is discovering our purpose in life. So, even if we pile heaps and heaps of material possessions around us, at the end of the day, all those possessions cannot fill the emptiness we still feel inside."

"That's right. And, once we realize that the emptiness is still there, we come to the painful discovery that our material quest did not give us the answers we sought."

"Then it seems logical that we move into one of the other quadrants on the spiritual side."

"That's what happened to me," replied Robert, "I embarked on my first real attempt of defining myself in spiritual terms."

"I would assume that most people do that by looking to an outside organization, like a church, a religion, or a cult, to provide all of the answers they need," Bill commented.

"That's been my observation. Like most people I looked to organized religion. Ended up following what I was told blindly, and hoping that this 'external spiritual' source would be able to give me the answers I was after."

"From the look on your face I can tell that you didn't get the answers you were looking for."

"No, I didn't. But I can only speak about my experience. I'm sure that many people have found ongoing benefit from their association with organized religions. And for many people an intense and devout relationship with their religion of choice is the right thing for them. It wasn't for me."

"Was the experience of any benefit?" asked Bill.

"Absolutely. I freely acknowledge that this part of the journey, the experience of beginning my spiritual search through organized religion, was extremely useful. It made me ask fundamental questions about what I knew, or thought I knew, and forced me to question the validity of blindly following religious dogma."

Robert's hand touched his chest as he spoke, "I know I have a jaundiced view of organized religions because of my experience. I have to apologize for that. But from my perspective, I found that they had lost sight of the true intent of their mission. They had become more interested in expanding their power base, and filling the collection plate, than in helping people find the answers to their spiritual quest. It appeared to me that many were totally consumed by their desire for self-perpetuation and domination over their competitors rather than acting as a conduit to higher spiritual consciousness."

"It's not fair to brand all religions that way, Robert. There's a tremendous amount of good that various churches and faiths do around the world. Especially in supporting the poor and championing human rights."

"I know that intellectually, Bill. It's just that there are so many examples of where the Bible, Qur'an and other religious writings have been re-written, or at least interpreted, in ways to suit the whims of quasi-religious leaders that I find it hard to get past that point. The terrorist attacks on the World Trade Centre and the Pentagon in the name of Islam are absolute perversions of that faith. The politicization of religion is a dangerous global trend."

"That may be so," said Bill. "I think most people realize that the recorded history of mankind is full of conflicts that were started and perpetuated on religious grounds. Many people would agree that irrelevant points of religious dogma have led to the deaths of millions of people around the globe. For all we know, millions more may continue to die in the future. But that doesn't negate all of the good work that is done around the world by various organized faiths."

Robert smiled warmly and shrugged his shoulders, "I warned you that I had a jaundiced view. I'm still struggling to find a way to forgive all of the suffering that has happened on this planet in the name of religion, especially when the core beliefs of all of them are identical. To me, the entire situation is like a giant comic tragedy."

"I don't understand how you can say that all religions are the same."

"I think it was Aldous Huxley that researched every recorded culture in history. He found that virtually all of them, regardless of their origins, had three core beliefs. The first was that there is another place beyond earth. The second belief was that a part of that other place resides in all of us. And the third was that the purpose of life on earth is to get to that other place. That's all there was. Sure the terminology was different: Heaven, Nirvana, soul, bliss and so on. But, when we strip away all of the dogma, almost all cultures and their religions are left with those same three core beliefs."

Bill was intense, his brow furrowed. "Okay. Let's move on a little bit. I accept that from your experience, organized religion, this 'external spiritual' state as you call it, wasn't the answer for you. Your diagram would logically now lead to the 'internal spiritual' quadrant. So, you feel that we'd move there because we tried the material routes with no success, and then found the 'external spiritual' to be self-serving on the part of the churches. Therefore the only thing left is to go inside our selves. Is that where you feel the answer lies?"

"That's what I thought when I went off on that part of my journey. I was like many people and tried to find the answer to my search by going inside myself through meditation. It was a very appealing place to be since I could shut myself off from the rest of the world. It was quiet and peaceful. There was only one problem; meditation is a self-centred activity. In a way it is the ultimate egocentric activity. It kept me in one realm and shut me off from everything else. I was shutting myself off from life and I was missing the lessons that were being made available to me by the Universe."

Bill started to shake his head, "I have to admit that this is getting pretty bizarre Robert. We've gone through all four of these stages on your diagram and we still haven't found the answer. We've just gone around in circles. This is a bit frustrating."

"You're right, Bill. And, it was extremely frustrating to live it out too. I found that before I moved from one stage into another there was a period of disillusionment. A realization that I didn't find what I was looking for. After I entered and re-entered the various stages often enough, I tried to stand back from the entire process and view it in a larger context. But I couldn't force any understanding to come. It had to come to me of its own accord. Which it did."

"Interesting comment Robert. If you're talking about an experience that allows you to see the world from a higher level of consciousness then you could have experienced a mini-satori or perhaps a full-blown satori, depending on exactly what happened."

"You'll have to explain that, Bill. I've never heard of a mini-satori. I'm not sure I fully understand what a satori is either."

"In eastern religions there are seven levels of consciousness. Level one is simple physical matter of all types. The second level is where we develop as a biological life form and have an emotional and sensational connection to the Universe. Level three is equated to our intellectual development. There are three sub-stages in this level, culminating with the full integration of our physical/emotional/sexual being with the mental/intellectual aspects of our mind-body existence. Very few of us even get to level three. It is at the fourth level that mini-satoris occur. The fourth level is sometimes referred to as the 'dark night of the souls' since the altered state of consciousness it represents makes a person much more sensitive to senses such as smell, touch, hearing and sight. It can be a period of sensory overload and can be dangerous as the spiritual traveler may acquire extraordinary powers. Phenomenon such as channeling, ESP, telepathy, astral travel, and other paranormal displays are often associated with this level. It is at this level of consciousness that people get their first glimpse or fleeting awareness of the infinite energy of the Universe. This small flash of understanding of the vastness of this power is a mini-satori. Some call it experiencing a truth or 'the awakening of the psychic heart'. At any rate, it is an insight that alters our perception of how we are connected to the Universe."

"Fascinating," said Robert as he studied Pearce. So where do satoris fit in?"

"Full-blown satoris are most often associated with the practice of Zen. They take the spiritual traveler through levels five, six and seven of consciousness. A satori is a sudden, unexpected flash of insight into the real nature of the Universe, or of the nature of man. In the Zen tradition the first satori is the personal experience of a loss of self and the recognition of a no-thing-ness, a void. The second is the realization that to have an experience of any kind, even of a no-thing-ness or void, means that one has not truly escaped the self, since one is still conscious of experiencing something, even if it is a void. So, this second satori is the realization that the first satori was an illusion, a trick that the Universe played on us. The third satori is where the traveler crosses over and is no longer an experiencer of any kind, nor are there any experiences to be had. There is only, as it is said, an unchanging stillness that comes from being one with the Universe."

Robert thought for a few moments. "I can't relate to any of these three specific satoris that you have described. What have your experiences been like?"

"If you're asking whether I've ever personally experienced a satori or mini-satori, the answer is not yet. At this point I'm just a student of the theory."

"Well, based on your descriptions I'd have to say that my experience appears to be a mini-satori. Something more connected to the fourth level of consciousness."

"Interesting. What insight did you gain?"

"It was at that point that I learned that I had discovered a

great deal about my journeys through the four quadrants I
described to you. I knew where not to find the answer."

"So where did you look?"

"I came to the realization that I didn't have to look."

"Why is that?"

"There was no need to look. By discovering that there was
no place to go for the answer, I learned that I already was the
answer. I already was what I sought. I already was that other
place described in all the recorded religions of the world. I
already was part of God, if that's the term we want to use to
describe this other place."

Pearce's eyes narrowed, "Where are you going with this
Robert?"

"Mankind created religion thousands of years ago because
we could not deal with the concept of physical death. We needed
something to comfort us, to reassure ourselves that there was
something else after we were through with our bodies. So, we
invented symbols and stories that the common man could
understand and take comfort in."

"Are you suggesting that the Bible, Qur'an and other
religious writings are not valid?" Pearce asked.

"No, I think that they can have great personal validity for
many people. It's all in how people use them. These writings can
help lead people to a higher level of spiritual awakening and
enable them to lead more compassionate lives. On the other
hand, the writings have been interpreted in ways that encourage
readers to become more judgmental of others and promote
separateness and elitism."

"This gets back to the notion you raised earlier about
organized religions loosing sight of the spiritual journeys of their
members and being concerned more with promoting themselves
and growing their congregations."

"Let's remember that the personal use and interpretation of
these religious writings is a choice. There can be a big difference
in being spiritual and being religious."

"So how much spiritual truth do you think is in these various religious writings?"

"Let's just say that at the time these writings were created the average person was not able to understand abstract concepts, especially metaphysics. The great mystics and spiritual teachers of the time used parables and created images that were easily recognized and understood by the populace to try to explain metaphysical experiences and Universal truths."

"You're suggesting that some of the stories in these writings were invented as convenient methods of teaching. Some people might brand you a heretic for having such views, Robert."

"Perhaps. If some people want to label me they will. I can't control that."

"As a popular author that doesn't bother you?"

"You mean do I worry that they might stop buying my books if they label me in a negative way?"

"Yeah."

"Not really. They have that option now regardless of what I might say or write. It is more important that we are true to our spiritual journey rather than just simply focusing on making money while we're here."

"When you say journey are you talking about our religious or spiritual beliefs?"

"What we believe is not relevant to the Universe and our experience of it, Bill. Beliefs are seductive, but cheap."

"That strikes me as a harsh comment. Why do you say that?"

"Beliefs seduce because they are easy, ready-made answers. They are cheap because they leave no room for doubt about how the Universe works and our place in it. The absence of doubt leads to an absence of spiritual growth. All too often we simply regurgitate what we are told within a particular religious context, and often there is no requirement for us to live our lives any differently...only believe. Beliefs insulate us from having to experience the Universe as individual cosmic wanderers, lost and alone. This is where real personal courage and spiritual growth is found. Living our lives within hard cast beliefs is choosing to live in a bubble. Deep inside every 'true believer' is the nagging fear that something will come along to destroy his or her cherished ideas, to pop their bubble. That's why belief systems, religious and otherwise, have led to book burnings and pogroms in the past. Anything that threatens a true believer's bubble must be destroyed, or at least repressed."

"But what do we have without beliefs?" Pearce asked. "Entire societies have existed and operated for hundreds, even thousands of years based on beliefs."

"And have those beliefs allowed us to live in peace and harmony over that time?"

"Point well taken, Robert."

"The only things that matter are what we have come to truly know through direct, experiential understanding of the Universe. These things are authentic and come from being touched by the Universe. A group of people huddled in a cave for their entire lives can believe in the existence of the sun, but they have not experienced it. Their social and religious norms may dictate a belief that the sun is purple and cold and will kill them if they leave the cave. They do not *know*. Someone outside of the cave, who has seen the sun and experienced its warmth, *knows*. That person does not have to claim any belief in the sun. They have experienced the sun. They *know*."

"Isn't that what the Bible, Qur'an and other religious writings try to do? To share Universal truths which have been experienced by those that wrote the passages?"

"Absolutely. The intent is good. The problem is in the translating of these overwhelming spiritual experiences into words so that the people in the cave can understand. For the writer it was a knowing. For the men in the cave it will always be someone else's knowing. It can never be their experience. Imagine what would happen if a person who has experienced the sun goes into the cave and tells the people inside about the sun."

Pearce thought for a moment. "Well, it's pretty obvious that the person from outside would probably get a negative reaction since his or her experience is a direct contradiction of the beliefs of the people in the cave. The cave people would probably resist adopting his experience of the sun into their belief system."

"Are the cave dwellers likely to leave the cave so they can experience the sun first hand?"

"If we assumed a high degree of socialization around the belief had occurred, it would be extremely unlikely that any of them would leave the cave," Bill answered. "Going out to experience the sun would be equated to committing suicide under the original belief system."

"Even though someone from outside the cave can attest to the true nature of the sun?" Parnell asked.

"Sure. That person is still an outsider to the cave group. Their experience could be interpreted as the ranting of a madman. Now, if one of the original members of the cave group went outside and then came back in and described the sun they would have more credibility. Whether the group or some individuals would risk going outside would still depend on the strength of their individual beliefs and the group pressure to conform."

"If a few of them did choose to leave the cave would their experiences of the sun be identical?" Robert asked.

"Not necessarily. Each could have a different level of sensitiveness to the sun. Some of them could get badly sun-burned from the exposure. Others may not. Each could see the colour of the sun differently. They could be wearing different amounts and types of clothing which would cause some to become hotter than others."

"That's my point Bill. Truth is individual. The only truth that is relevant to you is your truth. Not someone else's. Truth is like an airline ticket with your name on it. No one else can fly on your ticket, and you can't fly on anyone else's."

"Can I get you a drink gentlemen?"

Parnell and Pearce were broken from their discussion by the flight attendant's question.

"Ah...sure. A cola please," Bill replied.

"Make it two," Parnell added.

Pearce smiled at Robert. "Can't say that most of my airplane flights have had discussions on this level."

"Me either. Nice when it happens though." Robert tried to collect his thoughts for a moment. "Must admit I'm having some trouble trying to get back to the original point we were discussing before we got on our discussions about beliefs."

"Satoris," Pearce replied. "You were explaining an insight that came to you."

"That's right. It was the realization that I already was what I was seeking. That I already was part of the other place talked about in various world religions."

"Already being a part of God. Seems a bit out there, Robert."

"There is some grounding for this notion in modern theoretical physics."

"How so?"

"Einstein's general theory of relativity suggests that matter and energy are one in the same. Matter is simply congealed energy, and energy is simply released matter. Many theorists of quantum mechanics suggest that the only difference between matter and energy are the vibration speeds of the particles. Some even go as far as to theorize that solid matter may be composed of nothing more than light rays that are sort of frozen into particular patterns. If we follow Einstein's thought that matter and energy are the same, then there is no difference between my life energy, my thought energy, and the body that I find myself in. They are interchangeable, depending on their vibration frequency. If our bodies and life energy vibrate at dramatically different frequencies they could project themselves into dramatically different dimensions simultaneously."

"So, what are you trying to tell me, Robert?"

"Concurrent existence. We exist in two different energy dimensions at the same time. We are here in this physical realm as well as in that other place that all the religions of the world have talked about for centuries."

He stared at Robert. "Concurrent existence? How and where did this realization come to you in the mini-satori you experienced?"

"I can't say where it came from because I don't know. What I can tell you is how it came and revealed itself to me."

"Well, you've got me this far, you had better continue."

"I was driving in my car on the way to a client meeting when I had a very strange physical sensation come over me. It was like walking around with no skin over my muscles and having someone sprinkle salt on my exposed flesh. It was an incredibly heightened sense of awareness."

"Sounds like you experienced a stage of level four consciousness," said Pearce. "There is often a heightening of the physical senses. Then what happened?"

"While I was in this state images appeared in my mind. I became a molecule of water. It was fascinating! I went everywhere that a water molecule could go, in and out of animals, plants. I evaporated and became a part of rain clouds and fell on other areas and had other adventures as I was transformed through all living things on land. These images were flashing through at an unbelievable rate of speed. I lived all of the images that were in my mind. Since all the images that had come to me were linked to the land, to fresh water, I heard myself asking if this was all there was. Suddenly I found that I fell as a raindrop into the ocean. I then lived the entire experience as salt water, becoming fish, kelp, sea mammals, and birds, everything that exists in the oceans of the world. Then I started going from one realm into the other. From salt water back to fresh through evaporation, and then falling into the other realm as a rain drop."

Bill Pearce watched Parnell in amazement. Robert was in a

trance-like state, reliving the entire experience in his mind.

Parnell continued, "Fundamental questions came to me. I asked myself if this was all there was? Being on land or in the ocean? Being in one state or the other? Is there only one place where we can exist, or was there a possibility to be in both places at the same time? The next thing I saw was myself falling as a raindrop on some distant shore. Falling at the exact spot where the salt water of the ocean and the land met. At that precise moment of contact I was in both realms at the same time, the land and the sea. Then I realized that there are an infinite number of these places around the globe. Millions of miles of ocean shore lines, river banks, lake beaches."

Robert came out of his trance-like state and turned to Pearce. "It was at that point I knew that we existed in two concurrent realms. I knew that we existed here in this physical world, and also in another totally different but connected energy plane."

"Sufi mystics often talk about two different states, Baka and Fana. Baka is an awakened consciousness of an individual and the five senses, and Fana is a higher form of consciousness where the individual no longer exists." Bill explained. "In the Sufi tradition the highest state of man is when we are able to balance between these two states. Was the truth that came to you similar to that?"

"I'm not sure. I haven't been exposed to Sufi writings and traditions so I don't know enough about their views to comment intelligently. What I came to know from this experience is that we live in two different energy realms concurrently. Our inspiration and creativity often comes from this higher energy plane, as do our moments of 'ah-ha' when a deep understanding of the Universe overwhelms us. We are both 'here' and 'there'. The challenge is that we don't realize that we are in the 'there' because a cosmic fog usually hides it. These two energy dimensions are both here and now."

"Robert, I don't quite follow what you are trying to tell me."

"All I know is that I've tried to explain this experience to a few other people, but I've never been able to do it. It's been so frustrating and makes me feel so alone. Whenever I try to explain it I get blank stares in return. I'm sure some people think I'm on drugs or that I've simply lost my marbles. I've come to accept that all I can do is continue on my journey and use my work to leave some markers along the way. Hopefully they'll help other people find their way."

"How has this revelation helped you?"

"It puts our everyday life here into a much broader context when we know we exist in parallel dimensions. It's much different than believing something because beliefs often crumble when challenged. When we know deep down at our core that there is much more than this physical realm we are more open to accept the lessons that are presented to us here. When we know that our life energy exists and continues beyond this realm there is a feeling of clarity and balance."

"How do you ever hope to get people to understand what you've just told me about concurrent existence? You already said that truth is individual. That the only thing of relevance to me is the truth I experience. Not the ones you do."

"I doubt that I ever can. They will need to experience it in their own way, in their own time. Maybe the best I can do is simply let people know that I had this experience, so if they have one, at least they will know that they are not alone. I find the greatest challenge in writing and speaking now, is to try and be at the same place in the journey that my audience is. To try and relate to them in their sense of reality, not mine. Sometimes it's very, very difficult."

"But you're still going to keep trying?"

"I don't see what else I can do."

Bill Pearce studied Robert intently. There was no doubt in his mind about Robert's commitment, his sense of purpose, and the absolute honesty in the way he had described his experiences. He put his hand on Robert's shoulder. "If you ever think you've discovered a way to help the rest of us find this understanding, this Universal truth that has come to you, I want you to call me. I don't know what I can do but I'd like to help."

CHAPTER 8

Stephanie took in a deep breath through her nose, smelling the rich aroma of coffee. She glanced up at the clock noting that it was almost eight-thirty. As she continued to prepare breakfast she couldn't stop her mind from drifting back to the conversation with Laura the previous night. As she relived the discussion about Laura's father she was overwhelmed with emotions: anger, shock, pain, revulsion. The graphic pictures in her mind sickened her, but at the same time, she was struggling with competing emotions. She wondered what tormented Laura's father and what pressures were brought to bear on him that would lead a man, a father, to hurt his child. She questioned if he ever regretted what he did or if he ever understood the reasons behind his actions.

Laura entered the kitchen just as Stephanie was setting the table.

"Food smells great Stef," said Laura yawning, "I slept like a log."

"Good, you needed it. It was a tough evening for you."

"Thanks for being there for me Stef. It's the first time I could ever talk about it with anyone."

"Laura, I don't want you to feel any pressure to say more about it if you're not comfortable. I'll be there for you whenever you need me."

Snider closed her eyes and nodded as Stephanie served their plates. The two women sat down to eat and started to reminisce about their lives in California, their discussion was warm and spontaneous. After they finished eating Stephanie began to clear the table.

"So what do you want to do today?" she asked.

Laura shrugged her shoulders, "I don't know. Any suggestions?"

"How about a tour of the city?"

"Sure. Are we still on for pizza tonight?"

4 Ounces to Heaven

"Uh-huh. I've got an idea," said Stephanie as she placed some dishes on the counter top and opened a cupboard door, retrieving a thick telephone book. "Let's browse though this and see what strikes your fancy."

She flipped to the restaurant section and angled the book so Laura could view the pages. As they looked over the advertisements Laura pointed one out.

"This might be the place I ate at last week," she said.

"Ambruzzo's. I've never eaten there. Was the food good?"

"Terrific! Besides, there are some questions I'd like answered about a certain bartender."

"It's on the south side of town so we can make it the end of our tour. Probably best to make it an early dinner too. I'm not sure but I think it's in a pretty rough area. I'll call to see if we need reservations."

"Ask if the owner has a huge gray moustache, then we'll know it's the right place."

Stephanie confirmed their reservations for six o'clock and the moustache. "So what would you like to see in Chicago today?"

"I've only been here a couple of times before but I didn't do much sightseeing. What would you recommend?" Snider asked.

"Chicago is a fabulous city. There are forty-six museums. Over two hundred theatres. The Harold Washington Library Center is the world's largest public library with over two million books. And, some of the world's tallest buildings are in the city," Mendoza replied.

"You sound like a tour guide."

"I should. I had a part-time job doing the commentary on a city bus tour," chuckled Mendoza.

"Really?"

"Sure. Needed the money. Rookie doctors don't make much."

"Well let's hear your best tour guide stuff then," Snider challenged.

Stephanie cleared her throat, and then began her verbal tour. "Chicago is a city rich in history. It was first settled in 1779 by Jean Baptiste Point DuSable a fur trader of French-African decent from Santo Domingo. He established a trading post on the north bank of the Chicago River. Twenty-four years later Fort Dearborn was built on the opposite bank. The area continued to grow and in 1833 Chicago was incorporated as a town, then into a city in 1837 with a population of over four thousand people. The city became a major transportation hub in 1848 when the Illinois and Michigan Canal was completed, linking the city with the Mississippi River. Business blossomed and the population of the city tripled during the following three years. The famous Great Chicago Fire started on October 8, 1871. It ravaged the west side of the city and soon spread. Two days later it had claimed over three hundred lives, left ninety thousand homeless, and destroyed over $200 million in property. The Chicago River is the only river in the world that flows backwards. Engineers reversed it in 1900 for sanitary reasons."

"Slow down a little!" Snider pleaded. "You weren't kidding about the tour guide job!"

"You were the one that asked for my best stuff."

"That I did."

"Want more?"

"Just a little. Give me a few more facts. But make them trivia that I can use for fun when I get back home to L.A."

"Okay. Here's a few 'firsts' for Chicago. Roller skates in 1884. A steel frame skyscraper in 1885. An elevated railway in 1892. Cracker Jacks in 1893. The zipper in 1896. The Hostess Twinkie in 1930. The world's first controlled atomic reaction happened at the University of Chicago in 1942. And, the first McDonald's restaurant opened here in 1955."

"I had no idea. Since I've only been here a few times in the past all I really relate to is O'Hare and Navy Pier."

"This city almost bursts with pride. Did you know that the

University of Chicago has had more Nobel Laureates connected with it than any other institution? Speaking of O'Hare, it started in operation in 1955 and Navy Pier attracts about seven million visitors a year…"

Laura threw up her arms in a mock surrender, "You win! Take me for a tour. I am at your mercy great guide of the city!"

After spending the day seeing some of the sights of the city the women arrived at Ambruzzo's just before six.

"I'm absolutely starved!" Laura said. "All we had for lunch was a hot-dog from that cart vendor. How do you keep up such a crazy pace without food?"

"Sorry. I guess after a few years of working long, crazy shifts at the hospital my body is used to an irregular meal schedule."

As they entered the restaurant Tony Ambruzzo recognized Laura immediately. "So the lovely lady returns! Was it the food or Tony's singing?"

Laura laughed. "Both Tony. I'm surprised you remember me."

"It's not everyday I see Todd in such beautiful company," replied Tony as he motioned for the women to follow him to a table, placing menus on it and pulling out their chairs.

"Is there anything I can get for you?"

"We don't need menus, I know exactly what I want," said Laura.

Tony beamed. "So do I," he said as he bounced off to the kitchen.

"What was that about?" Stephanie asked.

"I just ordered our dinner."

"How? By mental telepathy?"

"No, by family tradition."

Within a few minutes Ambruzzo reappeared carrying a pitcher of beer and a plate of bruschetta. "Your pizza will be ready in a few minutes."

Laura's eyes quickly scanned the restaurant. "You're not too busy yet Tony. Do you have a couple of minutes to sit and chat?"

Tony reached for one of the chairs from a nearby table, responding to her request.

"Tony, when I was in last week I noticed your cookie jar by the cash register. I heard a little bit about Sean's Club at a presentation at the convention centre and I had to come back to ask you about it."

Ambruzzo's face grew serious, "You know about Todd's father?"

"Yes."

"Sean's Club is named after him."

"I thought it might be."

"When Sean O'Brien was in my arms that night, dying, I promised him that I would look after the children. Policemen don't make that much money so I knew it would be hard on the O'Brien family." Ambruzzo's eyes started to cloud over. "When another man gives his life so you can live, you can't waste your life. If you did it would make his death meaningless. So I helped the family as best I could. Then I found that there were many other children in the neighborhood who were in need." Tony clasped his hands together. "Money can help take away a child's hunger, or shield them from the cold, but that's not enough. The children in this neighborhood needed hope. They needed to believe that they could have a better life than what they saw around them."

"So you started Sean's Club for them?"

"Yes for them, and for Todd's father. I wanted people in the neighborhood to remember him and what he stood for in this community."

"Robert Parnell talked about Sean's Club during his speech last night."

"Robert is a special friend. He often comes to the club when he's in Chicago. He has helped so many children."

"Was Todd one of them?"

A wisp of a smile flashed over Tony's face. "Yes, he helped Todd a great deal. The money we raise for Sean's Club goes toward many things. We have programs to help get kids off the streets and away from crime and drugs. We give them counseling. We arrange to put some of them through technical training so they can find jobs. Some we support by paying for higher education."

"How did Parnell help Todd?"

"Sometimes we find exceptional kids, like Todd. And we know we need to invest more in them, because they'll return it to the community. That's where Robert helps out. He sponsors kids going after post graduate degrees."

A broad smile lit up Tony's face as he continued. "Todd was the youngest person to earn a Ph.D. in psychology at the university he attended. Robert sponsored him."

Laura's jaw dropped. "But, Todd's a bartender."

"Todd is many things," said Tony. "He tends bar a couple of shifts a week. He does volunteer work at Sean's Club. And he also owns one of the most sought after performance consulting groups in the country."

"So that's how Parnell came to Chicago. Todd hired him to speak through his performance consulting company," said Stephanie.

"That's right," said Ambruzzo. "Todd uses some of the profits to help finance Sean's Club and other things in the community." Ambruzzo glanced around the room, seeing that it was beginning to fill. "If you will excuse me, I have many tables to serve."

The two women continued to talk after Tony left, Stephanie wanting to learn more about O'Brien.

"So you met Todd at a bar?" she asked.

"He was the bartender at the hotel the first night I arrived in Chicago. As a rule I don't work conventions, but I learned that if you're in a strange town it's important to make friends with the bartenders at the hotels. They always know what's going on at the hotel and they'll tip you off if they know the vice squad is on the property. Last Tuesday I was in a party mood so I put a move on Todd. He ended up talking me into pizza here at Tony's and then catching some blues at a local club. It wasn't at all what I had in mind."

"So how was your evening?"

"It was a lot like being in high school again. Todd was right off-the-wall. I was never sure what he was going to do next. But he has a way about him that made me feel relaxed being around him. He made it easy to forget who I was."

"So what do you remember most about the evening?"

"He drove me back to the hotel. I guess it was nearly one in the morning and I asked him up to my room to spend the night. He turned me down flat so I got defensive. I thought it was because of my line of work."

"That wasn't the reason?"

"No, he looked me straight in the eye and said he wouldn't expect to go to bed with any woman on a first date."

"How did you react to that?"

Laura shook her head as she looked down at the table, "I guess I blew up at him. I thought he was just giving me a line."

"What happened next?"

"Basically, he said it was my choice whether or not I believed him. Then he thanked me for the evening and tried to give me a good night kiss."

"Tried?"

"Yeah, I wouldn't let him. I turned and stomped off to the elevator. I was so steamed that when I got up to my room I threw some of my things around. I called him every name under the sun and then I sat on the corner of the bed and cried."

"You cried?"

"Yeah. I realized that I couldn't control the situation with him like I was accustomed to doing. I mean…other guys are just stiff hunks of meat. They pant and drool like dogs in heat. I can get them to do whatever I want. Todd wasn't like that. He treated me like a real person. It was the first time in a long time I could remember being treated like that. It scared me. I didn't know what else to do."

CHAPTER 9

At seven AM Robert Parnell entered his study for the first time since returning from his road trip. It had been a grueling eighteen days, ending with his presentation in Los Angeles. As was his custom after a long trip Robert dedicated his first two days back at home to Joanne, his wife of thirty-two years. They found joy in the minutia of life: going for long walks each morning, sharing thoughts over a pot of tea in the afternoon, and cuddling in front of the fireplace in the evening.

As he sat down behind his desk he saw the results of Joanne's presence. All of the mail that had arrived over the past twenty days was neatly placed in one of the three coloured file folders. The blue folder was marked 'Read/Discard'. The green one, 'For Signature'. The red folder, 'Special Attention'. Next to the telephone sat a printed summary of calls Joanne had fielded in Robert's absence. A brief description of each conversation was noted, along with pertinent details about the caller. Any follow up action required of Robert was highlighted with a yellow marker.

He scanned the yellow highlights on the telephone summary list and marked the time of each of his planned return calls. Next, he removed the large elastic band that surrounded the bulging green folder in which Joanne had placed the replies she had prepared to the numerous letters that had been received over the past several weeks. Robert read each letter and corresponding reply then signed his name to each. He returned the reply letters to the folder and snapped the elastic back around it.

It was almost nine o'clock when Joanne appeared at the doorway, two steaming cups in hand.

"I made some tea and thought you might like one," she said, placing one cup on the desk in front of Robert and putting a three-ring binder down. "Do you want to review your schedule?"

72

Robert reached for his cup and smiled, "I just got home and already you're trying to get rid of me again!"

Joanne was used to his teasing and winked back, "You're like a bad penny. I couldn't get rid of you if I tried."

He looked over the next three months of the schedule. "It's nice to see that there's no more marathon road trips coming up. This last one was a real killer."

Joanne sipped her tea then pointed to the red folder, "You got an air courier package from Chicago. It arrived the morning before you returned home from Los Angeles. You may want to spend some time with it."

Robert was puzzled as he opened the file folder, picking up the letter that sat on top of the small stack of papers inside. He looked at the letterhead.

"What's Winterhaven?"

"A hospice in Chicago."

Parnell's expression became intense as he read the letter.

Dear Mr. Parnell,

I hope this letter has found it's way to you. Since you probably receive thousands of requests every year, I must admit that I feel awkward asking you for your help. There are so many people with great needs.

Yesterday evening I had the chance to attend your speech at the convention centre here in Chicago and I cannot adequately put into words how much your message touched me.

Our facility attempts to provide care and comfort to AIDS patients. When you showed the circle diagram and spoke about how we are made up of three parts, I couldn't help but see the faces of the eleven patients in our facility and the hundreds of others that came before them.

AIDS sufferers have a badge thrust upon them by society because of their illness and are condemned and reviled by many people. They enter each day helplessly watching their bodies waste away and go to sleep wondering whether they will awaken in the morning.

They need to know that they are more than their bodies and more than the name of the disease that ravages them. They need to know about their being. Their life energy.

Gaining this understanding will help them deal with their deteriorating physical condition and help them cope with the callousness of people who treat them as outcasts. It will enable them to define themselves differently, so that when it comes time to leave this world, they can do so the same way they entered it; in dignity and without fear.

Mr. Parnell, I realize that you are a busy man but I hope you can find it in your heart to visit us during your next trip to Chicago. Our patients desperately need to hear your message.

Sincerely,

Greg Osbourne
Director, Winterhaven

Robert's face was expressionless as Joanne watched his eyes flash across the letter a second, then a third time. Finally he looked up at her.

Joanne reached into an envelope on her lap and dropped two sets of airline tickets on Robert's desk. "How would you like to take a little break tomorrow and go to Chicago with me?" she asked.

CHAPTER 10

As the Parnell's entered the arrival lounge they were greeted by Greg Osbourne, shaking hands warmly.

"I'm so glad you could come to Chicago again so soon. It's a pleasure to meet you," said Osbourne.

"The pleasure is ours," said Joanne.

"How was your flight?"

"Smooth and uneventful. Just the way I like them," replied Robert.

Greg smiled, "We can all be thankful for that. Especially given recent events." He glanced down to their hands then continued, "Winterhaven is only a twenty-five minute drive. I assume you checked your bags."

"We travel light," said Joanne, "No bags."

"When are you going back to Toronto?" asked Osbourne.

"Tonight, on the eight o'clock flight," she replied. "We're here to visit the people at your facility."

Osbourne was stunned. "I…I never thought you'd make a special trip here just to visit Winterhaven."

Robert put his hand on Greg's shoulder. "Your letter touched us both very deeply, Greg. We're here to do whatever we can to help."

On the way to the hospice the Parnell's learned about the history of the facility. It was privately funded through donations and staffed almost entirely by volunteers and had been operating for nearly twenty-five years.

"When Winterhaven originally started we handled terminal cancer patients almost exclusively," explained Osbourne. "We're located in a poor community where most families can't afford basic medical care let alone an extended hospital stay. Our facility was critically needed. About eighteen years ago as the HIV infection spread through the local area we shifted our focus."

"Where did the name Winterhaven come from?" asked Joanne.

"Being from Toronto I'm sure you know how cold and lonely winter can be for many people. That feeling of cold despair, of isolation, is common with the terminally ill. We wanted to create a place to shelter them."

"A haven," said Joanne.

"Exactly," replied Greg. "We just put the two words together. It took a lot of effort from the community, but we raised the money to convert an old three-story walk-up. The rest, as they say, is history."

When they arrived at Winterhaven Joanne and Robert met some of the staff, volunteers and patients.

"There are two bedrooms per floor with each accommodating two patients," said Osbourne. "There's also a bathroom and a small waiting area per floor which makes handling nature calls far more convenient and provides more privacy when visitors come to see patients."

The Parnell's went from room to room meeting and visiting with the Winterhaven patients. Robert spoke to each one at great length, forming instantaneous bonds with them, drawing out their fears, frustrations, and unfulfilled dreams. Robert spoke to them about their real nature, their energy. All the while, Joanne was at his side, caressing and comforting the patients' emaciated bodies, and offering them encouragement.

By late afternoon they entered the last bedroom. It was on the third floor and faced the street. One bed lay empty, its former occupant having passed away on the previous evening.

Joanne gasped as she turned and saw a tiny shape in the other bed. The child was so thin the outlines of the bones in her arm were clearly visible. Her face was drawn, the hollowness of the little girl's cheeks contrasting sharply with the angled appearance of her lower jaw. The small head turned toward Joanne, its enormous blue eyes sparkling.

"Hi, my name is Sarah."

Joanne moved over and sat on the edge of the little girl's bed. "Sarah, that's a very pretty name and a very old one. It comes from the Bible."

"I know, that's what my mommy told me." The enormous blue eyes looked up. "What's your name?"

"My name is Joanne. Joanne Parnell, and this is my husband Robert." She motioned for Robert to come over to the bed.

Robert grabbed a chair from against the wall and moved it to the head of Sarah's bed.

"Do you have any kids?"

Joanne caressed Sarah's forehead as she spoke, "No sweetheart, we don't."

"Why? Don't you like kids?"

"We love children very much," said Joanne as she leaned in closer to Sarah. "I guess God just thought that it would be better if other grown ups became mommies and daddies instead."

"That doesn't sound fair to me."

Robert smiled warmly as he moved his chair in closer to Sarah, "Well, it's okay Sarah. At least we get to meet special little girls like you."

"Do you like to play games, Mr. Parnell?"

"You don't have to call me Mr. Parnell."

"Yes I do."

"Why?"

"Because my mommy said that was the right way to do it. She said to always said mister."

"Can't you just call me Robert?"

"No." Sarah slowly moved her head from side to side, emphasizing her statement.

Robert thought for a few moments. "Sarah do you know what a compromise is?"

"I think so. It's like a deal. It's when you both kind of get what you want."

"That's exactly right. How about if we make a deal, a compromise, and you call me Mr. Robert? That way you get some of what you want and I get some of what I want?"

Sarah pondered the offer for a few moments then finally agreed. "Okay, I'll call you Mr. Robert."

He stroked his chin with his hand. "Now, I wonder what we could do for fun?"

"Games!"

"Oh yes, games! What's your favourite, Sarah?"

"I like Connect 4 the best."

"Connect 4? I never heard of that game," said Robert, "Do you have it here?"

"Yes, its in the box on the table." A pencil thin arm extended and pointed toward the corner of the room.

"Would you like to teach me how to play?" asked Robert.

"Okay!"

He brought the game over to her bed. "So tell me Sarah, how do we play Connect 4?"

"First you pick which coloured pieces you'd like, black or red. Then we take turns putting them in the yellow holder. Whoever gets four in a row first, wins."

"Four in a row. Sideways or up and down?"

"Sideways, or up and down, or on an angle."

"Hmmm, this sounds like a tough game. My guess is you're pretty good at it."

Sarah's smile sparkled almost as much as her eyes. "Do you want to have a game Mr. Robert?"

"You're on!"

As they started to play Joanne and Greg left the room, going to the waiting area to sit and talk.

"Greg, that little girl, Sarah. Sometimes life is so unfair," said Joanne shaking her head.

Osbourne spoke quietly. "Her parents are both dead. Father died last year, mother about six weeks ago. I first met them when they were fourteen year-old runaways living on the streets. By sixteen they were shooting up and turning tricks for drug money. Both contracted HIV, probably from sharing needles. Sarah was born HIV-positive, her mother was nineteen at the time. Sarah's nearly seven years old now. Sometimes I think it's a miracle she's lived this long."

"How did she get to Winterhaven?"

Greg sighed, "Getting pregnant with Sarah really straightened her mother out and she went to a community drop in centre looking for help. Luckily some local counselors intervened and helped get her off drugs. They tried with the father but he just bounced back in and out of programs for a couple of years. He couldn't keep clean so Sarah's mother broke off the relationship. She got some skills training and was able to work for almost four years before the disease started to take her. Sarah's symptoms became noticeable at about the same time. All of the hospices in the area were full, but because we have a good relationship with the drop-in centre they called us, and Sarah and her mother both eventually ended up here."

Osbourne looked at Joanne, his eyes clouding over with emotion, "Sarah's a brave little soul. I've never heard her complain about what's happening to her. There's something in her eyes. They're so alive! They just don't seem to belong in the rest of the package."

Joanne got up and peeked into Sarah's room. "They're both still at it. Is there any place we can get a coffee?"

"Sure, come on downstairs and I'll make some."

As Joanne and Greg talked over a cup of coffee, Sarah and Robert Parnell were finishing up their last game.

"I told you this was a tough game," said Robert as he put the game pieces back in the box. "You beat me three times!"

"Maybe you'll beat me next time, Mr. Robert."

"Well, I just might little lady. You had better practice."

Sarah's giggle seemed larger than her body. As she settled her huge blue eyes looked up at him, "Mr. Robert, do you ever get scared?"

He held her hand as he spoke, "Of course I do, Sarah. Everybody gets scared sometimes."

"I get scared when I think about my mommy. She's gone.

I know I'm here because I'm going to die soon."

A lump grew in Robert's throat, forcing him to swallow hard to fight back his emotions. He gently stroked Sarah's hair. "Sweetheart, we're all going to die someday. Did your mommy ever tell you about Jesus?"

"Yes."

"Well, then you know that the story of Jesus teaches us that there is a place people call Heaven. Its another place where we go after we die here and that's where your mommy is."

"Is that where I'm going to go?"

Robert nodded his head in agreement. "Yes, Sarah. I'm sure that's where you'll go."

"Will I like it there?"

"I think you'll find out that it's a magical place, Sarah. Do you like flowers?"

"Uh-huh, I think they're very pretty."

"Well, I think Heaven will be like a giant field of flowers. All fresh and colourful. It will be full of wonderful smells from all the buds and you'll be able to hear birds singing. There will be beautiful butterflies fluttering all around."

"Do you really think it will be pretty like that?"

"I think it will be even more pretty than that."

"When I get there I'll be sure to tell you what it's like Mr. Robert."

Parnell felt his emotions rising, "I'm sure you will sweetheart."

As Sarah reached up Robert bent over and gave her a hug. "I wish you could stay here with me," she said, "Then I wouldn't get scared. You make Heaven sound so nice."

His mind was racing as he held Sarah, trying to find the right words to comfort her. Finally, he ended their embrace and looked into her huge, blue eyes. "Sarah, you know that I can't stay here with you?"

Her quivering lips answered Robert's question.

"I think I know a way that part of me can be here with you

all the time. Whenever you feel a little scared I'll be here to talk to you. Would you like that?"

Sarah nodded.

Robert held her hand as he spoke. "Good. I'm going to ask Mr. Osbourne to take me out for a little while and I'll be back with a special gift for you. I promise that before Mrs. Parnell and I go back home tonight I'll make sure that part of me can stay behind with you. Okay?"

Sarah reached up to hug Robert again. He held her close. "It'll be okay, Sarah. You won't have to be scared anymore."

He sat up straight and motioned to the door, "I'm going to find Mrs. Parnell now. I'll ask her to come upstairs and visit with you while I go out for a few minutes with Mr. Osbourne."

Just before he left Sarah's room Robert turned, "Sarah, make sure you play Connect 4 with Mrs. Parnell and don't you dare let her win."

"Don't worry Mr. Robert, I won't," Sarah replied with a smile.

Robert found Joanne and Greg chatting in the kitchen on the ground floor of the hospice. After giving her a hug he asked that she go upstairs to visit with Sarah.

"Greg, is there an electronics store in the neighborhood? I want to go out and buy a small gift for Sarah."

"Sure, there's one about four or five blocks away. I'll get my coat and I'll walk over with you."

The men returned within twenty minutes, a long, rectangular box under Robert's arm and a plastic bag in his other hand. After hanging up his coat, Robert asked Osbourne if there was a quiet place in the hospice where he could go and not be disturbed. Greg took a 'Do Not Disturb' sign off the inside of one of the bedroom doors and then pointed Robert toward the bathroom on the main floor.

He smiled sheepishly, "I hate to say it, but that's probably your best bet. I'll ask the rest of the staff to use the other facilities for the next little while."

Robert took the plastic bag and the long, rectangular box and headed for the bathroom. About twenty minutes later he emerged and went upstairs to the third floor. As he entered the little girl's room he found Sarah and Joanne still playing the game Connect 4.

"You didn't let her win did you?"

"No," Sarah said proudly, "She didn't win any games, just like you."

Joanne winked at her husband as she got up from her spot on the side of the bed.

He looked down at Sarah, emptied some of the contents of the plastic bag on her bed, and then opened up the long, rectangular box as he spoke, "I told you I was going to leave part of me behind, and here it is." He handed Sarah an audiocassette tape and placed a portable cassette player on the bed next to the little girl.

"I've recorded a special message for you on this tape so you can hear me whenever you want. And, you don't have to worry about the tape breaking because I made an extra one." He handed her a second tape. "See both of them have a label that says, 'A Gift to Sarah from Mr. Robert.'" He showed her the end of each cassette tape. "I took the end of a ballpoint pen and I broke off the little tabs that used to be here. That way you can't accidentally erase this message."

Sarah was beaming as Robert handed her a third cassette tape. "This last cassette tape is for you to make a message for me if you want to. That way I can have a part of you, just like you have a part of me."

"Can I play the tape now?"

"Would you mind waiting for a little while? I'd rather have you wait until Mrs. Parnell and I left for the airport. Would that be okay?"

"I guess so."

Robert sat down on the side of the bed next to Sarah and showed her the tape recorder. "See, this is a very special tape recorder. I put batteries in it so you can use it without having to plug it in, or you can ask Mr. Osbourne to use this power cord and plug it into the wall. The other thing that makes it special is that it has two sides to put tapes in. You use this side if you just want to play a tape. You put it in here and press this button. Or if you want to make a message for me one day all you have to do is put the blank tape in this other side. Then, you press the red button that says 'Record' and this button that says 'Play'. You just talk into this end of the tape recorder, into this small hole that has the shiny ring around it. Do you think you could do that?"

"I can do it," said Sarah confidently. "Do you want me to show you?"

"That's a good idea," Parnell said as he handed her the tape recorder.

Sarah put it on her lap. "When I want to play a tape I put it in this side. Close this door, and then press this button marked 'Play'."

Robert nodded his head in agreement, "Perfect."

Sarah smiled broadly. "When I want to record a tape I put it into the other side. Then I close this door." She studied the buttons on the top of the machine intently, "Then I press this one marked 'Play', and..."

"That's right. You're doing great," Robert encouraged.

"And...then I press the red button."

"Right. And where do you talk?" Parnell asked.

"Into this little hole on the end that has the shiny ring around it."

"Super. And when you are finished making your tape what do you do?"

Sarah looked at the machine, then back at Robert. "I don't remember."

"Do you know why you don't remember?"

"No."

"Because I forget to tell you! Silly me," Robert said as he stuck out his tongue and made his head wobble from side to side, eliciting a giggle from Sarah. "See this button on the very end?"

"Uh-huh."

"It says 'Stop'. When you're done recording you press this one. Then you can take your tape out."

"And break the tabs off. Right?"

"Only if you're sure you aren't going to use the tape again."

Sarah nodded her head in agreement and hugged the tape player to her chest. "Thank you Mr. Robert! I promise I'll take really good care of it! I'll make sure it doesn't get broken!"

Robert reached over and tussled Sarah's hair, "Oh, I'm sure you'll take very good care of everything, Sarah. I have something else for you."

Sarah's eyes sparkled, "What is it?"

Robert took a pad of white drawing paper and a set of coloured markers out of the plastic bag, and flipping up the cover sheet showed her a drawing he had done for her. It was a brightly coloured scene with a rainbow, flowers and butterflies filling the page.

"Oh, it's beautiful Mr. Robert! Look at all the flowers and butterflies."

"You can think of this as Heaven, Sarah. If you ever get lonely or scared, you can play the tape I gave you and look at this picture so you can imagine how beautiful Heaven might be. And someday, if you want to, you can draw me a picture, or write me a story. I even brought you some special envelopes you can use."

Robert removed some brightly coloured envelopes from the plastic bag and handed them to Sarah. "See, there's lots of different colours, so you can pick your favourite."

He glanced at his watch, then smiled down at Sarah, "Mrs. Parnell and I need to leave pretty soon so we can catch our airplane. Sarah, I promise that I'll stop in and see you every time I'm in Chicago. Mr. Osbourne has our telephone number so if you want to talk to me, or Mrs. Parnell, you can call us. I've already checked with Mr. Osbourne. He'll let you use the telephone in the office. But you have to make sure to ask first.

And Mr. Osbourne or one of the other people working here will dial the number for you. Okay?"

"I'll be sure to ask first."

"Good." He bent down and kissed her on the cheek. "I love you sweetie. I'll see you again real soon."

Joanne gave the little girl a warm hug and a kiss. Then she and Robert left the room, each pausing at the doorway to blow a kiss to Sarah.

Within a few moments Sarah heard the front door of the hospice open, then close. She strained to pull herself up to the window and watched the Parnell's get into Greg Osbourne's car. After the car drove out of sight she sat back in her bed and held the tape recorder close and reached for one of the audiocassette tapes. After opening the plastic case and taking out the tape containing the message from Robert, Sarah put it in the tape recorder and pushed the button marked 'Play'.

CHAPTER 11

Ａs their airplane taxied out onto the runway Robert and Joanne Parnell grew quiet. They both reflected on the day's events. Robert couldn't get Sarah's image out of his mind. Joanne thought about their whirlwind trip and her spontaneous decision to purchase airline tickets to Chicago.

She reached over and held Robert's hand. "You okay? You seem awfully quiet."

Robert looked at his wife and sighed. "Yeah. I'm fine. It's been a long day." He squeezed her hand, "Thanks for buying the airline tickets and coming with me today. It would have been a lot tougher without you."

Joanne smiled, "Hey, what are friends for?" She studied Robert's face as he returned to his reverie. "What was it in Osbourne's letter that made you agree to come to Chicago?"

He answered her with another question. "What was it in Osbourne's letter that made you decide to buy airline tickets?"

Joanne thought for a few moments. "There was an urgency in it. But it wasn't demanding. It was compassionate. There was an honesty, a directness that I found disarming. I just had this compelling feeling that we had to come here today." She looked at Robert and waited for a response.

He nodded his head. "I agree. But there was more than that. Towards the end I felt the words he used pulling at me. Like a huge hook had been thrust into my stomach." Robert reached into the inside pocket of his jacket and took out a folded piece of paper.

"You brought Osbourne's letter with you?"

"For some reason I just couldn't put it down. Listen to what he wrote at the end of it." Robert unfolded the paper and read from it verbatim. "It will enable them to define themselves differently so that when it comes time to leave this world, they can do so the same way they entered it. In dignity and without fear." Robert's thumb and index finger stroked the bottom corner of the letter. He repeated the last portion of the letter, "The same way they entered it. In dignity and without fear."

"You're thinking about Sarah?" asked Joanne.

Robert took a deep breath. "Yes, Sarah. She's so small and frail. And yet there is a real strength that I feel when I'm around her. She's so alive! Did you feel it today?"

"Yes, I did."

Robert looked up at the air vents overhead as he thought. "There's a reason why she's come into my life. I know it. I just don't know why." He raised his left hand to his head and stroked his forehead.

"Robert, you're trying too hard to find the meaning in all of this. Maybe we need to let whatever is supposed to happen, just happen."

"I don't think so." Robert looked at his wife. "You saw Sarah today. You saw how thin and frail she is. There isn't time. The reason she's in my life is right in front of me." He held out his hand, fingers extended. "I can feel the reason. It's out here. I can almost touch it!"

Joanne looked at him pensively. "You can't force these things, Robert. You know that. Maybe the reason already showed itself and you just missed it."

She thought for a few moments. "What did you put on the audio cassette tape?"

Robert reached into his jacket pocket. "When Greg told me I'd have to record her message in the bathroom I felt a little embarrassed to be in there talking to myself. So I wrote it out first, then recorded it." Parnell unfolded the paper and handed it to his wife.

Joanne took the note from her husband and began to read it to herself.

"Dear Sarah,

Although you have only just come into my life, I know that you are a special little girl...very special indeed. When I look into your eyes I can see so much kindness, so much energy, so much life.

87

If I were ever lucky enough to have a daughter, I would choose to have a daughter just like you.

I like the way you smile. I like the way you laugh. I like the way you hug me. I like the way you teach me games...even though you won't let me win!

Your mother was very proud of you today Sarah. And even though you couldn't see her, she could see you. She saw your smiles and they made her smile. She heard your laughter and it made her happy. She felt your hugs and it made her warm.

Your mother is waiting for you Sarah. One day you will feel her hold you again. You will see her smiles again. You will hear her laughter again.

She is in that place people call Heaven...that giant field of flowers I told you about. There are birds singing all around. Beautiful butterflies are fluttering in the breeze. And the air is full of the sweet smell of blossoms.

One day you will choose to leave us, Sarah. You will leave your body behind and you will go to that other wonderful place where your mother is waiting for you. And you will leave your fears behind, because nothing in your new home will ever hurt you.

And when you arrive, everywhere you look you will see the miracles of this other place people call Heaven...

Rather than steal, people will give.

Rather than hate, people will love.

Rather than destroy, people will build.

Rather than fight, people will play.

Rather than divide, people will unite.

Sarah, know in your heart that you will see your mother again. Know that when you choose to leave your body behind you will feel no pain. Know that your eyes will be dazzled by a new world of light and beauty. Sarah, know that you will be loved because you are Love.

Joanne sat silently. She read Robert's message to Sarah again, then handed the paper back to him.

"Well?" Robert asked.

"I feel all kinds of emotions swirling around. So many things strike a chord." Joanne's eyes were closed as she spoke. "But, I think the ones that really hit me were: choosing to go, leaving fears behind, and you will be loved because you are Love." She opened her eyes and looked at Robert. "Where did you get that line? You will be loved because you are Love."

"I don't know."

"Could that be it? Is that part of the reason why Sarah is in your life?"

Robert's gaze was fixed on Joanne. His eyes narrowed as he studied his wife's face. He bit his lower lip gently and nodded his head as if in slow motion. "You will be loved because you are Love", he said. "Yes, that has something to do with it. I can feel it now. It has something to do with how alive her eyes are. How gentle she is."

"What do you think you should do next?" asked Joanne.

Parnell closed his eyes and sat motionless. "I'm getting pictures of Todd O'Brien in my mind. I think I need to talk to him. I'll call him tonight when we get home."

CHAPTER 12

Todd O'Brien was preoccupied with the book he was reading and didn't answer the telephone until the sixth ring, picking up the receiver in his free hand and sandwiching it between his shoulder and ear.

"Hello."

"Todd? It's Robert."

"Robert! How are you? Sorry that I missed your speech at the Chicago convention centre a few weeks back. I got an urgent call from Atlanta."

"No need to explain."

"I hate missing you when you're in town. You don't get to Chicago that often."

"And you hardly ever get to Toronto."

"It has been quite a while. Must be three months at least."

"It's been too long." Robert paused noticeably then continued, "Todd, I need your help."

"You know you've got it. What do you need?"

"I'm not sure."

O'Brien laughed, "That doesn't sound like the Robert Parnell I know. That super-organized, focused, disciplined guy I know wouldn't make a call if he didn't know what he wanted. Are you sure you haven't been drinking big guy?"

"Todd, I know this sounds strange. I met a girl."

"Why you fifty-seven-year-old dog! Does Joanne know?"

"I don't mean that kind of girl or relationship. This is serious."

"I'm sorry Robert. I've got three months of teasing saved up."

"I met a little girl today in Chicago. She's about seven years old."

"Chicago! Are you in town?"

"No, I'm calling you from home."

"When did you fly in here?"

"This morning."

"And you're back at home tonight? This must be one special little girl."

Parnell sighed, "She's special alright. Her name is Sarah. She's in a hospice in Chicago called Winterhaven. She's dying of AIDS."

"Winterhaven? Now that's a familiar place. How would you find out about Winterhaven?"

Parnell was stunned. "How would I find out? How do you know about Winterhaven?"

"Well, sometimes the counselors at Sean's Club get involved with young people who drop in looking for help that we simply can't provide, especially from a health standpoint. We meet a lot of kids who are sick or are in real need of shelter. We try and help find them temporary accommodations and keep a register of the various shelters and hospices in the general area. When we get street kids in, the counselors refer them whenever possible to other organizations and groups that can help them. We haven't done that much referral work with Winterhaven since it's not really that close by and we don't often see terminal cases coming into Sean's Club."

"It's run by a man named Osbourne."

Todd's brow furrowed as he pressed his lips together, deep in thought. "Osbourne. Okay, I think I can place him. Is he a tall guy, mid-forties? I think his first name is Greg."

"Yeah, that's him."

"I've only talked to him three or four times over the past number of years. He's a very committed and compassionate guy as I remember."

As the two men continued to talk, Robert gave Todd details about the letter he had received from Osbourne, and went on to describe his trip to Chicago with Joanne and their visit to Winterhaven. He talked about Sarah at great length, filling in details of her parents and her current physical state.

"Her eyes are so alive, Todd. I can't describe what I feel

when I look into them. They have such depth, such energy, they seem out of place with her body. And because she's so thin and frail it makes her eyes look as big as saucers. I've been trying to figure out why she's come into my life."

"And that's what you need help with?"

"Yes. For some reason when we were flying home tonight I kept getting pictures of you in my mind. Todd, you're somehow connected to the answer."

"You said you bought her a portable tape recorder?"

"I wanted to help take away Sarah's fear, so I bought her a portable tape player today and recorded a message on it for her. I also gave her a drawing I did and left her some paper and markers. I wrote out the message before I recorded it for Sarah. Joanne thinks that part of that message points to the reason why Sarah's entered into my life."

"What was on the tape that Joanne thought was a clue?"

Robert took the note from his pocket, unfolded it and read it to Todd. "Three things in the message struck Joanne. The first was telling Sarah that she could choose to leave here. The second was that she could leave her fears behind. And, the last thing was that she would be loved because she is Love."

"She would be loved because she is Love?"

"That's the same phrase that struck Joanne. What do you think it points to?"

"She is Love. She is Love." Todd concentrated on the words, growing silent. He allowed his mind to wander as Robert waited patiently on the other end of the telephone. Soon Todd allowed his meandering thoughts to come out as words, speaking slowly and with clarity. His voice was soft and gentle. "Love is a perfect state. Where a perfect state exists, everything is in harmony. What do we call ultimate harmony? Eastern religions call it Bliss, Love. Christian religions call it Heaven. So, Heaven is a state of Love." Todd became centred again. "Are you trying to tell Sarah that she is a part of Heaven?"

Parnell's throat went dry, memories of the water molecule

vision that he had explained to Bill Pearce on the flight to L.A., crackled through his mind. "That's what it is! Concurrent existence! I need to show her that this other state, call it Bliss, call it Heaven, exists. Not only that it exists, but that she is already a part of it and that she doesn't have to be afraid of leaving here. But, how can I do that?"

Todd stared down at the book that he was reading when Robert called. "Robert, I think I have the answer in my hand."

"What do you mean?"

"I'm holding a book in my hand. It has the answer. We need to prove the weight of the soul."

"Weight of the soul? Where did that notion come from?"

"I'm holding a book on the life of Leonardo di Vinci. I've been reading it the past few days and I just finished a part that explained some of his more unorthodox theories. Robert, di Vinci believed that the soul had a physical weight and he theorized on how one would go about proving it."

"I've never heard that about di Vinci before."

"The man was remarkable. Almost unbelievably advanced for his time."

"Todd, I remember hearing stories about some obscure research that attempted to calculate the weight of the soul, but no one I know has been able to identify the exact source of those stories and whether they're true or not. I've tried searching various databases and the Internet and I've never been able to find anything. It appears to be here-say. An urban legend."

"Robert, who cares whether it's here-say or not? Suppose it was true. Suppose that it could be proved that the soul has a tangible weight."

"Then it would mean that the three common beliefs of the world's religions were founded in reality. That Aldous Huxley was right."

"How does Aldous Huxley fit into this?" Todd asked.

"Have you ever read about Huxley's research on organized religions? He found that virtually all of them had three core beliefs."

O'Brien thought for a moment, "I seem to recall something."

"Huxley discovered that virtually every religion had three core beliefs; that there is another place beyond earth, that a part of that other place resides in all of us, and that the purpose of being here on earth is to reach that other place."

"Now that I hear them, they do seem familiar to me."

Robert's mind was racing, "And, if we apply Einstein's general theory of relativity, it makes sense from a quantum physics standpoint. He theorized that energy and matter are the same, except that one is in a released form and the other is congealed. So, it stands to reason that when our life energy leaves our bodies there should be a loss of weight, because a loss of energy is the same as a loss of matter."

Todd interjected, "So, if we could actually demonstrate that there was a weight loss at the moment of death we may be able to prove the existence of the soul, or at the very least, that there is a measurable energy that provides the spark for our existence here."

"Exactly. And, we could prove that we exist in two different energy dimensions; that our life energy can be transferred between those two different dimensions. Scientists have long speculated that the Universe is in perfect balance, that the removal of even one atom would cause it to collapse in its entirety. Imagine if we could prove to the billions of people around the globe that we are all much more than just our bodies, that we are a Universal energy form."

"Robert, imagine what it would mean to people who fear death if they knew that they were simply leaving one dimension and that they would still exist in another. Imagine what a difference it could make on how people choose to live their lives here on earth, in this dimension. There are millions of people in this country, and hundreds of millions more around the world that goes through each day with an emptiness that eats at them continually. An emptiness that they try to fill with meaningless material possessions. An emptiness that they try to run away from with drugs and alcohol. But, if people knew that their existence doesn't end when they leave this dimension maybe they'd have a higher sense of purpose. Maybe they would be more compassionate. More understanding. More loving with each other."

"If we could prove that the soul exists it might be the catalyst for all of the religions of the world to come together and work as one. There would be no need for them to fight over arcane bits of religious dogma when the reality of the soul is staring them clearly in the face. Maybe people would stop stealing from each other. Raping each other. Killing each other. Maybe our species would finally learn how to truly love because we'd all finally understand that our presence here is a mere blip in our total existence and that our being here has a much higher purpose! We could all finally realize that we truly are spiritual beings having a temporary human experience here." Robert's heart was pounding. Sarah's image burned his mind. "Imagine what it could mean to a little girl waiting to die in a hospice in Chicago. Imagine how it could help take away the fear and the loneliness she feels."

"The possibilities are fantastic!" O'Brien added. "Imagine how it would help all of us deal with the fear and loneliness that virtually all of us now feel when we face death. Imagine if we could prove it to the skeptics, to the scientific community, that the soul exists. Imagine if the news spread across the globe and if all the peoples of the world learned that every one of us is made up of exactly the same energy. That the colour of our skin, the slant of our eyes, the name we call God, none of it makes any difference. Imagine the potential for tranquility, for peace, if we all stopped using labels on each other. If we became one in the human experience." Todd looked at the book in his grasp as his other hand moved up to the centre of his chest, stopping over a silver medallion hanging on a chain underneath his shirt. "We can do this, Robert. We'll need to get a team together. I have some ideas."

CHAPTER 13

It had been almost two weeks since Laura's chance meeting with
Stephanie Mendoza in the emergency room. She had accepted
Stephanie's offer to stay in Chicago and recuperate, finding the
rest was well needed. Snider spent the bulk of each day relaxing
and reading selections from Stephanie's extensive book
collection. During the past couple of days Laura had noticed
that she was starting to feel anxious, coming to the realization
that it was time to return to Los Angeles. But, she also knew she
couldn't leave Chicago quite yet and picked up the telephone,
punching in a number she had tried several times over the past
three days. After exchanging greetings with the voice on the
other end, she got down to her business.

"Is Todd O'Brien in today?"

"Todd? I know he's in, hang on a second. For some reason
I don't see him in the bar right now. Do you want to call back or
can I take a message for you?"

"I'm an old friend from out of town. I'd like to surprise
him. What time does his shift end?"

"Let me check the schedule for you."

Laura bit her lower lip as she waited for the voice to return.

"I'm probably not supposed to tell you this but the schedule
shows him out of here in about an hour and a half. Ten o'clock."

"Thanks very much. I'll see if I can make it over tonight.
Do me a favor and don't tell him about this call. You'll spoil the
surprise." Laura hung up the telephone. For the past couple of
weeks she had struggled with her feelings about seeing Todd
again. She wanted to know more about him than the details
Tony Ambrusso had supplied. She decided to shower and
change. After doing her makeup and hair she called a taxi to take
her to the bar, leaving a note for Stephanie to explain her
absence.

Laura arrived about nine-forty-five. Todd's back was facing
her as she entered the bar and she took a seat at one of the stools.

He heard the stool scrape on the ceramic tile floor and turned in response to the sound.

"Can I help...you!" A huge smile broke across his face. "I was hoping I'd get the chance to see you again. Back in Chicago so soon?"

"Never left. I've been visiting with an old friend for a couple of weeks. Do you have anything planned when your shift's over?"

"No, nothing planned. I've got a few things to do first thing in the morning so I can't stay out too late."

"How about a chat over a cup of coffee?"

"Sure, there's a nice little spot just a couple of blocks down the street so we could walk over. Or we could stay here and go to the coffee shop in the hotel. Want something to drink?"

"No, I'll wait for that cup of coffee."

"Do you want to wait here or in the coffee shop here at the hotel?"

"I'll just wait here. Then we can go for a stroll to the other spot."

After his shift ended Todd changed out of his uniform and freshened up. Then he and Laura walked over to the coffee shop, sitting in a small booth towards the back.

"So what have you been up to since I saw you?" asked Todd.

"Well, let me think. I got beat up, and..."

"Beat up! When?"

"A couple of days after I saw you. A client did it. I guess you'd call it an occupational hazard. It comes with the territory." Laura studied his reaction, and finding the look in Todd's eyes genuine and concerned, she continued, "I ended up in the emergency room of a large hospital here in town. The name of it escapes me. Anyway, after the ambulance guys wheeled me in I looked up from the stretcher and saw the face of an old girlfriend from California. Turns out she's a doctor at the hospital and works ER. I hadn't seen her for five or six years."

"How badly did you get hurt?"

"A few cuts and scrapes on my face, nothing too bad. I got a cracked rib and some swelling and bruising, but nothing that some rest couldn't fix."

"Sounds like you were pretty lucky. Thank God it wasn't too serious. Was this girlfriend turned doctor someone you met when you first moved to California? I think you told me you were still in grade school when you moved from the mid-west."

"How do you remember that?"

O'Brien shrugged his shoulders and smiled, "I don't know. I guess I thought it was important."

Laura cocked her head to one side and studied him for a few moments. "Thanks for remembering," she said. "To answer your question, yes, she is someone I met when my family first moved to California. In fact, she was my very first friend and ended up being my very best one, too."

"Must have been great to connect again."

"It's been fantastic. I forgot how close we were. The nice thing is how quickly it all came back for both of us."

As they continued to talk over their coffee Laura told him about her friendship with Stephanie and how the two of them had drifted apart in their college years. She went into more details about her hospital stay and the time she had spent living at Stephanie's condo apartment.

"Stephanie took me to the convention centre to hear Robert Parnell speak. Why didn't you tell me about him, Sean's Club, your doctorate, and all that the last time I saw you?"

A broad smile broke over O'Brien's face. "Sounds to me like you've been to see Tony Ambruzzo too."

"Guilty as charged. I took Stephanie out for dinner at Tony's the night after we went to the convention centre.

"Let me guess…squid pizza?"

Laura chuckled, "Well, it is a family tradition." She paused noticeably, "Todd, why didn't you tell me earlier?"

"About the Ph.D., my business, and that stuff?" Todd peered into her eyes as he spoke, "I wasn't sure how you'd react to me if told you all of those details. I thought I'd come across as just another guy stroking his ego. I figured if you saw me as a simple bartender we'd have a better chance of opening up to each other as people. That was very narrow minded on my part. I should have given you a lot more credit. I'm sorry."

She accepted his explanation. "Well, you've heard about my life the past couple of weeks. How about you?"

"I had the most incredible experience two nights ago. It was almost eleven and I was at home reading a book about Leonardo di Vinci when the telephone rang. It was Robert Parnell calling me from his home in Toronto."

"Robert Parnell?"

"Uh-huh."

"I heard him speak about a week and a half ago."

"He's a terrific speaker."

"I know. He had nice things to say about you too."

O'Brien smiled, "I've been caught again haven't I?"

Snider winked at him. "That's okay. Go on about your conversation with Robert."

"He had been here in Chicago for the day visiting a hospice called Winterhaven. Robert met a little girl named Sarah there and was very moved by her." Todd's arm motions became animated as he spoke. "There is something very special about that little girl. Her eyes are so huge, so blue, they look so alive!"

"So you've seen this little girl named Sarah?"

"Yes. I went to visit the hospice yesterday morning and spent a couple of hours with her. There's something incredible I felt just being around her. A gentleness. A calmness. But, at the same time, there is this fantastic sense of energy. I can't explain it."

Laura's gaze was intense. She could feel O'Brien's excitement. "What did Parnell want?"

"He wanted my help. He was confused about the emotions he was feeling about Sarah. He felt that she had come into his life for a specific reason, but couldn't figure out what it was. For

4 Ounces to Heaven

some reason I had been in his mind, too. So he called."

"So, did you help him figure out why this little girl Sarah was important?"

"I was holding the reason in my hand."

Snider looked at him quizzically, "The book about Leonardo di Vinci?"

"Exactly. I had just finished reading about some of di Vinci's theories when Robert called. He told me about an audio-cassette tape message that he had recorded for Sarah. Something in that message led us to the reason." He reached across the table and grabbed Laura's hand. "We're going to try to prove the existence of the soul! We're going to try and measure the energy of life!"

"You're going to do what?" Snider replied incredulously.

"We're going to try to measure the weight of the soul. Einstein theorized that matter and energy are one in the same. The only difference is that matter is congealed energy and energy is matter that has been released. Our hypothesis is that if there is such a thing as a soul, or life energy, contained in our bodies, when it leaves our bodies when we die there should be some kind of corresponding loss of weight."

"That sounds a little over the edge don't you think?"

"I know it sounds strange at first, if not totally bizarre. But the notion is not new. Throughout the ages many mystics and sages have said that the heart was the seat of the soul, or 'Atman' which is the self. Some have gone so far as to state that it lies about two inches to the right of center in the upper half of the heart. A few have even speculated that it weighs thirteen ounces."

"You realize how totally bizarre that sounds. I mean, there's not a shred of scientific proof for any of this."

"That's the beauty of this whole thing Laura. We're going to use the religion of science against itself, and have science prove the existence of something only thought of in spiritual terms before."

"What do you mean…the religion of science? It's not a religion. Science is based on hard facts and measurable evidence."

"That's what scientists believe and would like to have us believe. But think about it. Science doesn't really discover anything. Science is the business of inventing measuring devices."

"I don't follow your line of thinking."

"Let's say that a scientist somewhere has a hypothesis that something exists but it has never been measured before. Therefore in scientific terms it doesn't exist." O'Brien explained. "That's the dogma of science…if it can't be measured then it can't be real, it doesn't exist. There are so many obvious cases where something does exist but since scientists can't measure it they discount it totally."

"Give an example," Snider challenged.

"Spiritual healing in the Philippines."

"You'll have to explain that."

"For many decades, perhaps even longer, the Philippines have been home to a number of spiritual healers. Through these treatments countless people have made miraculous recoveries from aggressive cancers and all kinds of other illnesses. For many spiritual healing was their last resort since modern medicine had failed them. They are the living proof that this healing form does exist. Yet scientists remain skeptical because they haven't been able to explain what spiritual healers do, and how and why it works."

Laura was intrigued, "What exactly is spiritual healing?"

"It usually takes one of three forms: distance healing through prayer, the healer's hands on the body of patients usually holding the afflicted area, or putting the healer's hands into the body of patients."

"The healer's hands *into* the body of patients? You're going to have to explain that one."

"Leading scientific researchers have observed spiritual

healers, and filmed them, on numerous occasions kneading the skin of a patient until it opens up. Then the healer inserts their hands into the patient and draws out clots of blood and other substances. When this spiritual surgery, as it has been called, is completed the healer removes their hands and there is virtually no mark left on the patient."

"Fascinating. Their hands just enter their bodies?"

"Yes, usually wrist deep."

"That sounds unbelievable."

"Based on what we think we know of modern medicine and the human body it is. About twenty-five or thirty years ago scientists in Sweden and other countries subjected some leading spiritual healers to rigorous scrutiny under laboratory conditions and still could not determine how and why spiritual healing actually works. We have to investigate some higher levels of consciousness or look to theoretical physics for any kind of explanation."

"How does theoretical physics help to explain this phenomenon?" Snider asked.

"There is a growing body of opinion among theoretical physicists that our bodies may be composed of little more than light rays vibrating at a particular frequency. When the frequencies are aligned properly the effect is to make our bodies appear solid. If this actually is the case then spiritual healing may be a process where the healer is able to change his or her natural body vibration frequency to that of the patient's."

"So the entering of the hands could be as simple as two living organisms, the spiritual healer and the patient, vibrating at the same frequency and combining for a short time," Laura added.

"Absolutely. And for all we know cancers could be cells that are vibrating at the wrong frequency inside a particular body. When the spiritual healer enters the patient's body with his or her hands the effect could be to change the vibrations of the cancerous cells. This could explain why many patients' cancers disappear completely shortly after treatment. If we examine world religions, especially Eastern ones, there is some common belief that our journey to consciousness, to oneness with God, is composed of seven levels. The fourth level is the one associated with what modern science calls the paranormal. Perhaps people like these spiritual healers are simply further along the evolutionary path and can operate at the fourth level of consciousness at will."

"Still, the notion is so much out of context to what we think that it's very hard not to label these healers as little more than sleight-of-hand charlatans," Snider observed.

"No doubt there are some fakes out there, as there is with any profession. There are some that are absolutely genuine."

"How can you be so sure?" Laura asked.

"Three things. First, about ten years ago my best friend's wife had terminal cancer and was only given a few months to live. After several treatments with a particular spiritual healer her cancer completely disappeared within a couple of weeks. She's still alive today and doing incredibly well with no signs of the cancer. Second, there are some spiritual healers that have stood up to incredible public and scientific scrutiny for more than forty years. And lastly, I can't imagine a fake being asked to address the General Assembly of the United Nations, which one renowned spiritual healer did in the late 1980's."

"So, after all these years of skepticism and scientific scrutiny has anyone been able to quantify what these spiritual healers do?"

"In terms of success rate you mean?"

"That would be one way."

"Some spiritual healers are reported to be successful with seventy percent of patients."

"Really? Has anyone been able to determine how spiritual healing works?"

"In scientific terms?

"Yes."

"Nothing yet."

"Based on that I assume that scientists remain skeptical about this phenomenon."

"Totally. To them it is simply an unexplained phenomenon. The bizarre thing to me is that if some scientist invents a machine that can actually measure the forces at work during spiritual healing that scientist will be credited with 'discovering' it. Other than creating the measurement tool the scientist has no personal connection to spiritual healing forces, and no ability to actually do it. All the scientist would have done is invent a way of measuring it. Nothing more. 'It' already existed. Only the measurement of '*it*' didn't."

"I see your point. Tying this back to the project with Robert Parnell, what you're saying is if you can invent a way to measure a weight loss at the time of death you can present this quantifiable measurement as proof of the existence of the soul or the energy of life."

"Exactly. We'd need to link it to some of the theories of quantum mechanics that we discussed earlier, in order to present a plausible explanation."

"And you think you can do that?"

"I've been busy the past two days trying to formulate a project plan on how we'd do the measurements and the people we'd need on the project teams."

"What have you come up with?"

"We're going to use three hospices. Winterhaven in Chicago. One that Robert knows well in Toronto, and the one that Bill Pearce is familiar with in Los Angeles. They're sufficiently dispersed geographically to eliminate any possible challenges to the test results because of atmospheric or climatic factors. Each facility will dedicate one room to the project."

Todd took a pen out of his jacket pocket and sketched as he spoke. "An elaborate weighing platform will be set up in each weighing room. The platform is designed to weigh the patient, bed, and all the medical equipment that is in use at any given time. The total weight will be calculated on a continual basis and recorded digitally by a calibrated instrument that looks like a polygraph tester. It can capture and measure extremely minute changes in weight.

O'Brien looked up from his drawing to make sure Snider was following his explanation. She signaled her understanding so he continued, "At the same time as the weight is being monitored, the patient's heart and brain function will also be monitored on an ongoing basis. These readings will be graphed on the same recording paper where the weight is being recorded. The system will function on an integrated basis so we'll be able to see precisely what happens moment by moment on all three graphs right up to the time of clinical death and beyond."

Todd began to draw the floor plan of the entire test room set up. "In addition to the weight testing and monitoring brain and heart functions we'll also set up two digital video cameras in the room. One will be equipped with a wide-angle lens so it will capture the entire scene on a continual basis. The other camera will specifically record the movements of the three needles graphing weight, heart and brain measurements. These video cameras will be linked through a mixing board so they end up recording split screen on a master tape. The central unit will have a second master tape that will automatically switch over when the first tape has ten minutes left to run. That way we'll have an uninterrupted recording of exactly what happened every moment of every day. A small emergency generator will also kick in immediately in the case of any power interruption. The master tape will show an ongoing date and time code in the bottom corner."

"Why do you need to set up all this video equipment?"

"We want to ensure that the results of the tests are absolutely air tight in terms of verification. No one will ever be able to come back on us and claim there was something bogus about what we did or how we did it. To ensure that's the case the video cameras will be sealed as well as the master recording unit.

We'll have professional auditors break the seals and change the videotapes every six hours. Then they'll reseal the units and sign off on an auditor's verification statement."

"Sounds pretty thorough to me. How do you expect to get patients to cooperate?"

"It actually wasn't very difficult at all. I went to Winterhaven yesterday and talked to each of the patients individually. Robert and Joanne's visit really touched them. After they understood what we're trying to do they were eager to help out. They were all willing to sign participation agreements. All of them want to believe there's some place else after they leave here. For them to help prove that their life energy, their soul, is measurable, that it goes somewhere, gives them tremendous hope and purpose."

"What about Sarah? Did her parents agree?"

"She doesn't have any living parents. Both died of AIDS within the last year. Yesterday Robert talked to Sarah and her guardian on the telephone to explain things. Then I met with the two of them in person. It was amazing to see how quickly Sarah grasped what we're trying to do. She was eager to get involved and once her guardian saw how much it meant to Sarah, we got permission in writing."

"So when do you figure the patients would use the specially equipped room?"

"Their conditions will be monitored on an ongoing basis by physicians that are on site twenty-four hours a day. Once an attending physician feels that a particular patient is getting close to the end, say the last eighteen to twenty-four hours, they'll be moved into the Transporter Room."

"That's an interesting name for it. Who came up with that term?"

"The patients at Winterhaven got together and kicked around some ideas on what they'd want to call the room. It was Sarah that suggested it was going to be a space journey and getting transported into another dimension. She said it would be fun to go on an adventure like that. She was the one that mentioned going into the Transporter room."

"A Chicago version of 'Beam me up'."

Todd's eyes flicked up toward the ceiling. He smiled as he pictured the patient meeting in his mind. "You should have seen the shocked look on their faces when the suggestion came out of Sarah. They all just kind of sat there stunned and stared at each other. Finally one of them broke the silence, by saying the name was perfect. We helped him over to Sarah so he could give her a hug. It was incredible how this little girl restored hope in the others and helped change their fear of death into anticipation for a journey."

"I'd love to meet her."

"I'll take you whenever you'd like to go."

"I'd like that very much Todd. Maybe tomorrow afternoon." She raised her hand to her face and gently pinched her lips between her thumb and index finger as she thought for a moment. "Why are you doing this Todd?" she asked, "What's your motivation? I realize how this could help other people, but I'm not sure I understand what's in it for you?"

"You mean fame and fortune? I have all the money I need and all the accolades I can handle." He pressed his palms together, fingers pointing upward. "It's part of a long journey, Laura. I've spent over twenty years of my life pursuing, and trying to understand, the energy of life. This is another sign post along the way, another part of the adventure."

"The energy of life?"

Todd unfastened the top three buttons of his shirt. "I'm going to show you something I haven't let many other people see." He gave her a wink, "Now, don't be getting the wrong idea."

Within a few seconds he was holding a silver medallion in the palm of his hand. It was attached to a silver chain hanging around his neck. "I designed this symbol when I was seventeen years old, a few years after my father died. I was going through a very rough period at the time, struggling with his death and trying to figure out why he had to go. This symbol, and its meaning, came to me late one night. I drew it out on paper and had a jeweler cut it out of sterling silver for me. I've worn it every day since."

She leaned forward and extended her hand. Todd moved in closer to the table and placed the medallion in her palm. "So this represents the energy of life," Laura said. "Can I tell you what I see?"

"Sure. Go ahead."

"Well, the first thing is a circle. That's a Universal symbol for continuation so it must represent life, or the energy of life."

"You're right," Todd smiled. "Go on."

"There are three lines on the inside of the circle. They must stand for things that are inside life. Inside the person. Don't know what though."

"The top line is self-knowing. The bottom line is self-understanding. The line in the middle is self-being."

"Self-being in the middle." Laura thought for a moment. "I see the links. We have to know ourselves, and understand ourselves, before we can truly be ourselves." Laura studied the medallion for a few minutes. "I have no idea what these angles that radiate out from the circle are for."

"They're actually a series of six interconnected and overlapping triangles."

Laura stared intently, "Okay. Now I see them."

"They represent experiences we have in life that seem to be outside of our self-definition," Todd explained.

"When we go off on a tangent so to speak?"

O'Brien nodded his head in agreement.

"I understand. They're triangles because we bring those experiences back into our level of self-knowing, self-understanding and self-being. That's why the lines come back into the center of the circle. What about the two arrows that point in opposite directions? The Yin and Yang of life?"

"Yes. They represent any pair of opposing forces that we

encounter in our lives."

"So how do all of these things interconnect?" Snider asked.

Todd used his coffee spoon to point to various parts of the medallion and guide Laura through the next part of his explanation. "When we have these life experiences we just talked about, when we go off on these tangents…the triangles, we bring back important insights to increase our degree of self-knowing, self-understanding and self-being. As we bring these insights back we are able to thicken these three lines in the middle of the circle, our degree of self-knowing, self-understanding and self-being, until they eventually fill the inside of the circle."

"So what does that mean? Is our life complete? Have we found the meaning of our existence at that point?"

"No, not yet. But, we're learned enough about ourselves, understood enough about ourselves, that we can finally realize our talents and we can finally be who we really are. It's at this point we're ready to give ourselves to others and use our talents to serve them, to help them on their journey of self-discovery and meaning. And as we help others our own life energy expands until it touches all of the experiences in our life and all of the opposing forces that we perceive are in it."

"And then we understand the true nature of our existence?"

"Yes, that's when we finally realize who we are and our purpose in being here." He extended his hand so Laura could place the medallion in it. As Todd straightened up in his seat and let go of the medallion it swung back on its chain and came to rest against his chest. He buttoned his shirt.

"Robert is positive that Sarah is a key part of this quest we're on, he just doesn't know what part she'll ultimately play. She's quite weak so there's no real way of knowing how long she'll hang on. We're scrambling to get everyone we need on the three teams as quickly as we can. We still need another three or four doctors to volunteer for shifts at Winterhaven. Robert and his wife Joanne are quick workers. They've already got everything in place in Toronto. Los Angeles is our biggest challenge. Robert met a video producer named Bill Pearce on an airplane en route to L.A. Robert called him and told him about our project and he jumped at the chance to help out. Not only that, he spoke to a few hospice directors in L.A. and got one, Dina Lopez, to agree to have her facility participate with us. Bill's also volunteered to set up the video equipment in all three cities."

"How long will it take to get everything ready?"

"We should have all the weighing, monitoring and video equipment completely installed by the end of this week. The directors of each of the hospices are fully on board with the program, so much so that they've been calling other hospice directors in each of their cities to see if they'll participate as well by asking some of their patients to volunteer. As of three o'clock this afternoon we had a total of seventeen other facilities join in the program. That should give us sufficient volunteers to keep the three Transporter Rooms fully utilized most days. Broadening the number of participating hospices will also help to spread hope and purpose to many, many people."

"What if it doesn't work? What if you can't prove the weight of the soul, the energy of life? Won't that hurt the people who are participating by depressing them even more as they face their imminent deaths? That would be a cruel irony."

"It could. They know there's no guarantee that we'll be able to prove anything."

"Then why do it?"

"If we are right, the potential to help people gain new insights about the Universe is just too great to ignore. And, my gut tells me that I have to help Robert with this project."

"Because of what he did for you?"

"Yes, that's one reason," Todd replied. "The other one is that I need to continue on my path. Deep down inside of me I just know that this adventure has become part of my journey for a specific purpose. Somehow it will help bring me to a higher level of spiritual understanding."

"By proving the weight of the soul?"

"Yes, that could be a part of it," Todd said. "But, whether we can prove it or not, I feel that the experience of working on this venture will reveal a great deal to me and heighten my spiritual awareness."

"What do you think will happen?"

"I don't have a clue. What I do know is that even if we can prove the weight of the soul, simply discovering that new fact isn't going to be enough. Deep down I have a sense that the Universe will reveal things to me because of my involvement with Robert. How and why I don't know. I think the key is for me is to be fully absorbed in this project while suspending any and all judgments and expectations I may have about it. I have to release any thoughts that I might have about outcomes and simply surrender to the Universe."

"How does surrendering accomplish anything?"

"Surrendering allows us to be open to receive a message if one is supposed to come."

"What form does one of these messages take?"

"I don't know."

"There must be something that we can do in order to experience a truth. I've heard about people using mediation to get in touch with higher levels of consciousness," Snider commented.

"Maybe so. I suppose some people think they can do that. I don't believe anyone can meditate with the specific purpose of evoking a Universal truth. If it was that easy then we'd be much further advanced as a species."

"Why do you say that?"

"Once we experience a Universal truth our perspectives about life are permanently altered. It's like crossing a gorge on a rope bridge and then cutting down the bridge when we get to the other side. There's no way back after we've experienced a truth. The result is a deeper level of understanding and compassion. If we could simply meditate and receive a truth at will, then the world would be a much kinder, gentler place than it is right now."

"So you don't think there's anything we can do?"

"No, other than suspend our judgment and expectations about things."

"I'm used to being a little more goal oriented than that," quipped Snider. "I'm used to going out and getting what I want."

"Sometimes the more we push towards something, the more we tend to push it away. I think that's how it is with these moments of 'ah-ha'. They need to find us, rather than us chasing after them."

"You've experienced these truths before?"

"Just a couple of times."

"What's it like? How do you know when you've received one of these Universal truths?"

"I can only explain it from my limited experience. The first thing was that there was an overwhelming feeling of well being that rushed over me. At that precise moment everything around me seemed to be in perfect harmony and was seen with absolute clarity. It's as if the Universe whispered in my ear and I suddenly realized...Ah, so that's how it works! It was a moment of absolute calm and serenity while getting struck by something deep and profound about life or my connection to it."

"So what kind of specific experience or event happens to unlock a truth?"

"I don't think it has anything to do with the nature of the experience itself. It has more to do with seeing the world through a new set of eyes. Virtually anything that we do, come into contact with, or observe, could be the key to unlock a truth."

She studied Todd for a few moments, "Anything?"

"That's what I've read and heard from a few other people that it has happened to. It's a matter of timing and personal relevance. None of us is on the same path so what may be a sign post for you may mean nothing to me."

"Do these experiences have to be short in duration or can it be something you've been involved with for a long time?"

"Length of time doesn't seem to matter. What matters is

that the experience somehow is able to touch us differently at that instant. It's like seeing the same painting we've looked at everyday for years with a new pair of eyes, the truth was always there, we just didn't see it before."

"So why didn't we see it earlier?"

"Who knows? I like to think of the experience as going to view an oil painting at an art gallery. Let's say that every brush stroke on every painting in the art gallery was made from left to right, except one brush stroke on one painting was made from right to left. That one right to left stroke is the truth. It was always on the canvas, but we simply didn't look at that specific part of that particular painting very closely so we didn't notice it. With the thousands upon thousands of brush strokes on each painting, and the thousands of paintings in the art gallery it would be almost impossible to actually find it if we started a conscious search for it. Then, one day we are simply looking at that specific painting and that one brush stroke jumps out at us."

"Is it all really just happenstance? What if we have a special interest in that particular painting? We could look at it in detail and as a result stumble on that one stroke sooner."

"Intellectually that makes sense to me, but in my gut I'm not sure whether it would actually happen that way. I think it has more to do with the journey we're all on."

"How do we know where and when to start our journey?" Snider asked.

"The fact that you're here and alive is confirmation that your journey has already started. Your path reveals itself as you throw logic out the window and act on what your gut, your intuition tells you. It's a different kind of intelligence that lies dormant in most of us through neglect."

Laura's gaze wandered around the coffee shop as she thought. In a few minutes her eyes were locked with his. "I know a doctor who may be willing to help out here in Chicago."

"Your friend Stephanie?"

"Uh-huh."

"Great. When she's ready we'll introduce her to Greg Osbourne at Winterhaven."

"I'll chat with her a little more about it tonight. I'm going back home to Los Angeles in a couple of days. I'd like to be involved with this life energy project too. Maybe I could call Dina Lopez or Bill Pearce to see how I could help out once I get back home."

Todd's eyes clouded over, "I was hoping you'd say that."

CHAPTER 14

After finishing their coffee, Laura and Todd walked back to the hotel lobby, feeling very comfortable with each other.

"Do you need a ride back to Stephanie's condo?"

Laura looked at her watch, "It's getting pretty late and you have a meeting first thing in the morning. I think I'll just grab a cab. Do you think you'll have time tomorrow to take me to Winterhaven to meet Sarah?"

"No problem. Give me Stephanie's number and address and I'll give you a call at her place in the morning, say about eleven, to confirm."

"Sounds great, I'll talk to you then." Todd made no initial movement toward her so Laura extended her arms to embrace him. He responded, reaching out and holding her tight.

"Good night, Todd. Thanks for the evening." She kissed him lightly on the cheek.

After ending their embrace without any further contact, Laura went to the concierge to order a taxi. Todd waved and headed for his car and home.

Laura arrived back at the condominium just after one in the morning, and found Stephanie still awake.

"What time did you get back from the hospital?"

"About twenty after twelve. Want some tea?"

"Sure, thanks. How was work?"

"It was another brutal shift. We had so many patients in ER tonight I worked an extra couple of hours just to try and keep up with the influx." Stephanie looked exhausted, her eyes bloodshot and her lower eyelids dark and puffy.

"I hope your next shift isn't for a couple of days. You look like death warmed over."

"Thanks, I wish I felt that good. Next shift is later this morning, eight a.m."

"You'd better get to sleep then."

"Can't. Too wound up." Stephanie remembered the note

Laura had left for her. "How was your visit with Todd tonight?"

"Fascinating."

"Really. Why?"

"He's working on an incredible project with Robert Parnell and some other folks. They're going to do some research to measure the weight of the energy of life, the soul. I told Todd you might be willing to help."

"Yeah, right. I'm not sure I'm in the mood to talk about more work right now."

"I didn't commit you to anything. I just said that you may have an interest," Snider explained.

"So what are they doing?"

"They're working with terminal patients at a local hospice."

"Hmm. Probably cancer or AIDS."

"AIDS."

"You said that they're trying to measure the weight of the soul?"

"That's right, the soul, the energy of life."

"Sounds bizarre, but kind of interesting. How do they intend on measuring such an abstract thing?"

"They've got a very sophisticated monitoring system designed. Weigh scales, brain and heart monitors, and digital video recorders to capture the whole thing as it happens."

"What makes them think it's even possible?"

"Einstein's theory of relativity."

"E equals MC squared. I remember that from one of my university physics courses. The notion that matter and energy being one in the same, right?"

"Yes."

"And what makes you think I'll help?"

"I know you Stef. You've got a heart bigger than Lake Michigan." Laura went on to explain the research methodology in more detail, piquing Stephanie's interest and re-energizing her.

"If they could actually prove that we could measure

someone's life energy, their soul…" Stephanie shook her head slowly, emphasizing her words. "What an incredible discovery! Imagine how it could revolutionize conventional religious beliefs and scientific knowledge!"

"That's why they need to document everything so fully. They're expecting all kinds of people to come out of the woodwork to refute the entire project. By getting teams of professionals; doctors, medical technicians, auditors and the like, in each city, they hope to build credibility for the findings."

"How do you think I could help out?"

"They need to have volunteer doctors on-site at each hospice around the clock. Their job is to assess when patients need to be moved into the Transporter Room. At some point you'd also have to verify the actual moment of death. And, someone needs to help comfort the families. At Winterhaven, they're short three or four doctors."

"Hold on…Transporter Room?"

"It's the name that a little seven year old girl gave to the bedroom at each hospice that they're converting into the weighing labs."

"She's a patient?"

"Yes. Todd told me that there's something really special about her. Apparently this project was created as a direct result of Robert Parnell meeting her."

"Seven years old. She must have been born HIV positive."

"Uh-huh. Her parents were both street kids on the needle."

"How much time would I need to commit?"

"Shifts are three hours in duration. You can volunteer for as many shifts as you want."

Mendoza was pensive. "You know that you're sucking me into this don't you."

"What are friends for?" Laura said as a broad smile broke across her face.

"Well, I suppose I might be able to handle a couple of shifts a week. I'll have to police my hours at the hospital better. It would probably work if I put in a shift at the hospice before I started in ER." Stephanie paused, "Listen to me. I must be crazy."

"I was hoping that you would be. I'm going to help on one of the project teams."

Stephanie looked up and smiled, "Great! It would be super to work with you!"

"No, Stef. My team will be based in Los Angeles. I've decided to go back home in a couple of days."

Stephanie tried unsuccessfully to hide her disappointment. "Well…of course you're going back to California. Who's running the project out there?"

"The hospice director is a woman named Dina Lopez. She's looking after all the patient issues. A man named Bill Pearce is running the actual test centre set up in Los Angeles. He's also arranging the digital video for all three locations."

"Three locations?"

"Uh-huh. They plan to do identical weight tests in Los Angeles, Toronto, and Chicago."

"Why Toronto?"

"Parnell is a Canadian."

"Makes sense. What duties are you going to have?"

"It's not totally decided yet. I'll be calling Lopez and Pearce when I get back to L.A. to find out how I can help. Apparently their location is going to be the most challenging one of the entire project. As you can imagine there needs to be a lot of trust between our field teams and the various hospice personnel. Apparently Todd has good connections in Chicago, and Parnell in Toronto. That wasn't the case in Los Angeles. Bill Pearce, the man I mentioned before that's going to handle all of the video setup, only had contact with one L.A. hospice. One of Bill's employees was a patient in it. He passed away in the spring. Anyway, Bill has met with Dina Lopez, the hospice director, and she's agreed to participate. There's no formal team set up yet, so I suspect I'll have a mixed bag of duties."

"What about your regular line of work?"

"I've got enough investment income that I really don't have to worry about money. It will give me a chance to think about my priorities for a while. I think the timing is good for me to consider a career change."

Stephanie got up out of her chair, embracing her friend warmly, "I'm going to miss you Laura. It's been wonderful to see you again."

"Same goes for me, Stef. Don't worry. I won't be a stranger. I'll be back for regular visits. And you should come out to the west coast."

"I will." Stephanie glanced at the wall clock in the kitchen. "Time to hit the sheets. I've got to get up for work in a little more than five hours."

The women retired to their respective bedrooms. By the time Laura woke up the next morning Stephanie had already left for the hospital so Laura ate breakfast and got herself ready. She was looking forward to meeting Sarah and glanced at the telephone expectantly, wondering if Todd would be able to take her to Winterhaven that afternoon.

At eleven-fifteen the telephone rang. It was Todd confirming their visit to the hospice and that he would pick her up shortly after noon. He showed his usual punctuality, picking her up at ten after twelve. On the way to Winterhaven they stopped and bought lunch at a local diner, then continued on their way, arriving at Winterhaven just before two o'clock.

Greg Osbourne greeted them as they entered the hospice. "Todd, good to see you again", he said as they shook hands. "And this is?"

"This is my friend Laura Snider," O'Brien replied. "Laura, this is Winterhaven's director, Greg Osbourne."

"Pleased to meet you Laura."

"It's a pleasure to meet you as well Greg."

"What brings you back to Winterhaven so soon after your last visit?" Osbourne asked.

"Thought I'd visit with the patients again, and give Laura

the opportunity to meet our little angel upstairs."

Osbourne nodded his head and smiled, "Ah yes, Sarah. She is a little gem. Laura, try not to stay with her for too long today. She's getting pretty weak these days and needs as much rest as she can get."

"I understand. I'll keep it as brief as possible."

"No...no...I don't mean to rush your visit Laura. Sarah thrives on people contact. Just watch her closely and when she begins to tire you'll need to find a way to disengage from her gently."

Snider reached into her coat pocket and gave Osbourne a small piece of lined paper. "I have a friend who is a doctor here in Chicago. Here's her number. We talked about your situation here at Winterhaven and your shortage of medical volunteers. My friend Stephanie may be willing to help out. You may want to give her a call."

"Fantastic! Thanks so much Laura. I'll be sure to call her later today."

"Early evening is probably the best since she is working the day shift in ER today."

"Will do." Greg looked at O'Brien and Snider. "I have to slip out for a few minutes to run a quick errand. Todd, you know your way around. I'm sure you can give Laura the cook's tour, and then take her up to the third floor to spend some time with Sarah. I shouldn't be too long. Hopefully you'll still be here when I get back."

"Thanks, Greg. We'll see you later," Todd said, shaking Osbourne's hand.

✻

After a brief tour of the facility, Laura followed Todd up the stairs to the third floor to meet Sarah. She was lying on her bed as they entered her room. Sarah turned her head to greet them. Her eyes were so alive they almost sparkled. Laura looked at the little girl's wafer thin body. The contours of every joint and bone in her body were clearly visible, her cheeks sunken and sallow.

Sarah greeted them, "Hello, Mr. O'Brien. Who's your friend?" She could still manage a broad smile.

"This is my friend Laura Snider," replied Todd.

"Hi, Sarah. I've heard lots of nice things about you. I'm very pleased to be able to visit with you today." Laura sat down on the edge of Sarah's bed and stroked the young girl's hair. "Your hair is a very pretty colour."

"Yours too."

Osbourne appeared at the doorway of Sarah's room. "Excuse me folks. Todd would you have a few minutes to review the schedule for installing the balance of the Transporter Room equipment?"

"Sure. That will give you ladies some time to talk. See you in a few minutes." Todd gave Sarah a kiss on the cheek and left with Osbourne.

As the two men crossed the corridor to the Transporter Room set up at Winterhaven Greg explained, "We're almost a week ahead of schedule, Todd. Everything will be ready to test in a couple of days. If everything checks out we'll be up and running in three days."

As the two men looked at the first-to-be-completed Transporter Room they were both filled with a tremendous sense of anticipation.

"You know Greg, putting this project together has been the most exciting, all encompassing thing I've ever been associated with. I look around this room and I'm in awe of what we've done here. At the same time I can't help feeling that my guts are being torn out." He sighed noticeably, "People have volunteered the sanctity of their deaths to help us. I hope we won't disappoint their faith in us." He turned to Osbourne, "Do you think we should have done this? Do you think we'll be able to give them what they needed?"

"Come with me Todd." Greg grabbed O'Brien's elbow and led him down the stairs to the doorway of one of the patient rooms. "Look in there, Todd," Osbourne whispered, "Look.

Those are not the faces of people who have been crushed by a debilitating disease. Those are not the faces of people racked with fear. I see those faces and I see pride. I see dignity. I see peace. That's why we're doing this."

The two men embraced warmly. "Thanks Greg. Thanks for being willing to be a part of this."

"You'd better go upstairs and see how Laura is doing with Sarah. I'll be up in a minute or two."

As O'Brien reached the top of the stairs on the third floor he saw Laura leaving Sarah's room. Tears were streaming from her eyes. Todd felt panic grip his stomach. "Is everything alright? What's the matter?"

Snider rushed to his arms. "I need you to hold me for a while Todd. Just hold me."

He embraced her as she buried her face into his shoulder. He could feel his shirt growing damp with her tears. After a few minutes Laura regained her composure, looking up at him.

"Thank you for bringing me here to meet Sarah. I don't think I can put into words how much she has changed my life." Snider wiped the last of her tears from her cheeks. "Would you mind taking me outside? I need some fresh air."

As O'Brien and Snider went down the stairs they passed Greg on his way up.

"What's wrong?" Osbourne asked.

"Everything is okay. Better check on Sarah," replied Todd.

Osbourne bolted up the remaining stairs and entered Sarah's room, gasping in shock as he looked at her. As Sarah turned to greet him Osbourne could see that her eyes were iridescent, with colours bursting from them, lighting up the entire room in a kaleidoscope of patterns. His initial fear made him instinctively step back, swallowing hard. "Are...are you okay, Sarah?"

She smiled warmly. "Yes Mr. Osbourne, I'm fine."

He stared at her in awe. Sarah's eyes were still lighting up the room in a blaze of colours as she continued to smile at him.

He tried to regain his composure. "Is...is something wrong

with Laura? She was crying."

No Mr. Osbourne, she is very happy! She is crying happy tears!"

"Why is she so happy, Sarah?"

The colours continued to blaze from Sarah's eyes as she answered him. "Because we talked about why we picked our parents."

CHAPTER 15

Todd and Laura were standing on the sidewalk in front of Winterhaven when Greg came bursting out of the front door, visibly shaken. "Come with me I need to talk to you right away!"Laura and Todd exchanged puzzled looks as he brushed by them and walked briskly across the street dodging traffic. They followed him into a donut shop, and caught up with him at a table in the back corner of the store. He grabbed Laura's arm as soon as she sat down, making her wince from the pressure.

"Hey! Take it easy!" Laura struggled to get her arm free of his grip. "What's got you so cranked up?"

Greg looked at Snider his eyes were bulging wildly. "Sarah! Did you see Sarah! What did she look like when you were talking to her?"

"She looked like…I don't know…like Sarah. A little girl who is very ill," she answered.

"What about her eyes? Did you see her eyes?"

"Her eyes are beautiful. They're blue."

"You didn't see the colours? You didn't see the different coloured lights bursting out of them?"

"From her eyes?"

"Of course from her eyes!" Greg was shaking uncontrollably.

Todd moved his chair next to Greg and put his arm around his shoulder. "It's okay, Greg. It's okay. We believe you saw something. Try and settle down so you can explain what you saw."

He looked at Todd and nodded his head, taking a few long, deep breaths to calm himself down. "After Laura left Sarah's room crying, I went in to see what had happened. When Sarah turned around to look at me, her eyes were lit up like a Christmas tree! All kinds of different coloured lights were shining from her eyes. It scared the hell out of me!"

"What do you mean her eyes were shining?" Todd asked.

"Like I said, her eyes were shining! Light was coming out of her eyes! Coloured light!"

"What did you do?"

"I was so stunned I didn't know what to do, so I asked her a couple of questions, then left. I don't even remember what she said to me. I just wanted to get out of the room. She really freaked me out!"

Todd turned to Laura. "Would you mind staying here with Greg for a little while? I'll go back to Winterhaven and talk to Sarah." She nodded. Todd put his hand on Greg's shoulder. "Stay here with Laura for a while. I'll go see Sarah. I'll be back in a few minutes. You've been through something very powerful. It'll be alright, Greg. See if you can relax a little."

Todd left the donut shop and headed back across the street to Winterhaven. As he climbed the stairs to the third floor he was wondering what he'd find. Sarah heard his footsteps as he entered the room and turned to greet him.

"Hello, Mr. O'Brien."

"Hello Sarah. How are you feeling today?" He studied her face as he spoke. Nothing seemed out of the ordinary.

"I feel a little bit tired today."

"Oh. Did you have a good sleep last night?"

"I think so."

Todd bent down on one knee as he spoke to her, his left hand caressing her head. "Well, sweetie...why do you feel tired?"

Sarah shrugged her shoulders. "I don't know. I just do."

"Did you see Mr. Osbourne today?"

"Uh-huh."

"What happened when you saw him the last time?"

"He looked scared."

"Hmm. He looked scared did he? Do you know what might have made Mr. Osbourne scared?"

"No."

"Did anything strange happen in your room when he was here?"

125

"No."

Todd continued the dialogue and tried to get Sarah to open up. She kept on answering his questions with single word answers, refusing to offer any additional comments. After a few minutes Todd decided not to push the issue any further and kissed her on the forehead.

"Maybe you should try and have a little nap if you're tired, Sarah. If you rest up a little, you'll have some energy to play some games later. Would you like to do that?"

"I...guess so."

"You're not sure?"

"I want to see Mr. Robert."

Sarah's bottom lip was quivering. Todd watched a tear creep down her cheek and drop onto the top of her pajamas.

"Mr. Robert isn't here today, Sarah."

"When's he coming back?" Fresh tears began to form.

"I don't know sweetheart. Would you like me to call his house and find out when he'll be coming to visit next?"

Sarah wiped her tears with the back of her hand. "Yes, that would be good."

"Okay. I'll go downstairs and call him on the telephone."

"Tell him to come and visit."

"I will."

"Tell him he needs to come here real soon."

Todd's jaw began to drop slowly. Sarah's eyes were beginning to glow.

"Tell Mr. Robert he needs to come and see me. I have to talk to him. I need to tell him about the river."

"What river, Sarah?"

"The one that shines. The one I can see in my brain."

"Can't you tell me about it, Sarah?"

She shook her head. "No, only Mr. Robert."

CHAPTER 16

Joanne Parnell was just opening the front door of the house when the telephone began to ring, forcing her to hurry into the kitchen. She caught it on the fifth ring.

"Hello."

"Joanne, it's Todd. I'm at Winterhaven. Is Robert home?"

"No, he's in New York today."

"When's he coming home."

"Later on this evening. His airplane isn't even scheduled to land here until eleven so he probably won't be home until after midnight. Can I have him call you, Todd?"

"Where is he in New York? Can you reach him?"

She looked at her watch. "It will be difficult, he's probably on stage now. After that he has dinner planned with a client. I think his flight leaves New York about nine."

"Is there any chance he can change his routing and get into Chicago tonight?"

"I can try and find out. Todd, what's going on? I've never heard you so anxious."

"It's Sarah."

"Oh no! Is she...."

"She's still okay. She wants to talk to Robert. Joanne, Sarah became partially luminous today."

"What do you mean, partially luminous? You mean she started to glow?"

"From her eyes. She began to radiate light from her eyes."

"That's impossible."

"Joanne it's more than just possible. This phenomenon has been written about and documented for hundreds of years. Throughout the ages it's been reported that mystics have emitted various forms of glowing light from their bodies. Francis of Assissi in the twelfth century. Jnanseshwar, a yogi saint in the thirteenth century. Tukaram, a follower of Krishna, in the seventeenth. Seraphim, a Russian Orthodox priest, in the eighteenth.

And, most recently Krishnamurti in 1948."

She felt faint and sat down on a kitchen chair.

"Joanne? Are you there?"

"I'm still here. Todd, I just can't imagine that sweet, frail, little child glowing. These other people...when they started to glow...what caused it? Was it an initial stage before instantaneous combustion or something? Did they die?"

"No, death typically has nothing to do with it. All the material written about various luminous body phenomena indicates that these people would glow at times when they had significant spiritual revelations or insights. Some are reported to have glowed when they performed miracles of healing. They seem to somehow be connected with another energy realm or level of understanding."

"Do you think Sarah is somehow connected to another energy realm? I mean, what kind of spiritual understanding could a little girl like her have?"

"I don't know, but she says she sees a river in her brain. She wants to tell Robert about it."

"She won't tell you?"

"No, she insists on telling Robert. Can you reach him?"

"Let me look through the meeting file to see if I can find the number at the hotel in New York. Hang on a minute."

She went into Robert's study and pulled out a file folder from the filing cabinet and picked up the extension on Robert's desk. "I have the number here. I'll call the hotel and leave an urgent message for him to call me at home. Then I'll use the hot line with our travel agency to see if they can get him on an airplane to Chicago tonight. As a last resort I'll have him paged at the airport. We're bound to catch up with him somewhere this evening."

"Thanks, Joanne."

"Todd..."

"What is it?"

"I've never heard of people glowing. This is the strangest

thing I've ever heard. How can this be?"

"I'm not the right person to ask for a full explanation, Joanne. It could be related to a couple of things. We do know from laser research that when an electron changes from a high energy, excited state to a lower energy state that its atom will emit a photon which causes light to appear. So, Sarah's body could somehow be in a changing energy state."

"I can't imagine that."

"This luminous body phenomenon could also be linked to Einstein's theory of relativity.

"You mean how he theorized that energy and matter were one in the same, that energy is simply released matter, and that matter is energy that's stuck together?"

"Exactly. And Einstein also linked the speed of light into the equation. Remember, E equals MC squared? Energy equals matter times the speed of light squared. Modern theoretical physics has taken the relationship of light in the equation even further. Basically, some of the thinking now in quantum mechanics is that all matter could be composed of connecting light and electromagnetic waves, and perhaps other kinds of waves, going at a particular frequency or speed."

"How can a wave form something solid," Joanne asked.

"These waves move at a speed somewhat slower than the speed of light, in a kind of condensed state. The key is, that as an object increases in speed and approaches the speed of light, its internal speed and time actually slows down. In a way, the object would overtake itself when it travels at the speed of light, so at that instant, when the object is moving at the speed of light, time and distance do not exist. The object would simply convert into pure energy. At that point, the start and end of a light ray would not exist. Light would exist as a point of immediate contact. It would be a particle rather than a wave," O'Brien explained.

"So, what are you trying to tell me, Todd? Are you saying that our bodies are nothing more than light and other electromagnetic waves that are sort of frozen into a pattern? And that the only reason that they're frozen is because we're moving at a speed slower than the speed of light?"

"Exactly."

"So how do you explain Sarah's eyes glowing? She's not moving at the speed of light."

"Well, she doesn't appear to be from our vantage point, but she has to be tapped into something else, some other stream, some other energy. Or maybe her body speed is actually slowing down and emitting light just like a photon does in lasers. I don't know how this is happening."

"But the fact that she did emit light means she must somehow be close to a state where matter and energy become one. That strikes me as touching on a fundamental element of existence."

"If it's not the fundamental element of existence, it's got to be darn close. Joanne, we have to get a hold of Robert. We have to get him to Chicago tonight."

"Don't worry, we'll track him down and somehow we'll get him there tonight. When I track him down I'll have him call you at Winterhaven to let you know when he'll be getting in."

"Thanks, I'll pick him up at the airport."

Joanne put the telephone down. She closed her eyes and pictured the last time she had seen Sarah, remembering how she had told Robert that Sarah was so thin that she looked like a stick figure with eyes. To think of Sarah's frail body being capable of radiating light was almost incomprehensible to her.

She dialed the number of the New York hotel and left an urgent message for Robert. Then she called the travel agency and made arrangements for him to fly to Chicago. She tried to take her mind off Sarah by watching television but soon found herself on her feet pacing the floor, ending up in the study. She started to browse through the books on the shelves and within a few minutes selected one, and trying to calm herself, sat down to read. A half hour later the telephone on Robert's desk rang.

"I got your message at the hotel. What's wrong?"

"Todd called a little while ago. He needs you to go to Chicago tonight. It's Sarah, she…"

Robert interrupted, "Oh, no! Is she alright?"

"She's okay. Todd told me that she started to glow. She radiated light from her eyes."

"She…she radiated light?"

"That's what he told me."

"My God. Were you able to get me a flight?"

"You're on the eight-thirty. It's a direct flight into Chicago. You can pick up your revised ticket at the First Class check in when you get to the airport. Todd will pick you up at the airport in Chicago and take you to Winterhaven."

"Okay, I'll cancel my dinner. Can you call Todd back and tell him I'll be on that flight tonight?"

"Sure. When I was talking to him about Sarah I found it incredible that she could start to glow. He gave me some of the background on the phenomenon, calling it luminous body."

Robert was silent on the other end of the telephone, his mind racing.

"Robert? Are you still there?"

"Yes. Do you remember me telling you about the experience I had years ago in the car on the way to a client meeting? The one where I became a water droplet."

"That was the experience that gave you the knowledge of concurrent existence, the understanding that we exist in two separate but connected energy realms at the same time."

"That's the one." His voice trailed off.

Joanne could feel her husband's emotions surging through the telephone as she waited for him to continue.

Robert wiped a tear from his eye. "Joanne, that's why Sarah has come into my life! She's here to help me prove the existence of that other energy stream, to prove the existence of the soul. That the energy of life exists. Something tells me that's where the light is coming from."

CHAPTER 17

Robert Parnell rushed off the airplane and into the arrival lounge, finding Todd waiting for him.

"How is she?".

"She seems okay. She hasn't exhibited any more emissions since I talked to Joanne. I think Sarah's pretty scared, she clammed right up when I was trying to talk to her."

Robert put his arm around Todd's shoulder, "You can hardly blame her. Imagine going through what she has."

"Robert the strange thing is that she doesn't seem to even realize that she is emitting light. It's as if she is not even conscious of it. I think she's scared because of how we've been reacting to her."

"I've never heard of anything like this before," Parnell replied.

The two men got into Todd's car and headed off to Winterhaven. When they arrived, Robert tossed his coat over a chair in the front hall, and took two steps at a time as he raced up the stairs to the third floor.

Sarah was sleeping lightly as he entered her room and sensing his presence, she began to stir. He pulled up a chair next to the head of her bed just as she opened her eyes.

"Mr. Robert?"

"Yes, Sarah. I'm here."

"I'm so glad you could come." Her arms reached out to embrace him so Robert bent over the edge of her bed and held her tight, feeling the shivers running through her body.

"Its okay, sweetheart. Everything is going to be okay." He held her close and rocked her gently. After a few moments Sarah loosened her grip and Robert was able to pull away slightly so he could see her face as he spoke to her.

"Mr. Robert, I saw things today."

"Oh? What kinds of things did you see, Sarah?"

"A shining river."

"A shining river. It sounds like it must have been very beautiful."

"I'm not too sure."

"Why?"

"Well, I could only see a little bit of it."

"What did the little bit that you could see look like, Sarah?"

"It was very wide and the water was flat. There weren't any waves."

"Did you see anything else near the river? Any flowers? Or butterflies? Or trees?"

"No, just a river, a shining river."

"A shining river! That sounds very, very special Sarah. Did it shine any different colours?"

"It sort of sparkled some colours. But it was mainly white. It made me feel funny."

"Hmm. Mainly white. And it made you feel funny? How did it make you feel?"

"It tickled."

"It tickled! That sounds like a pretty nice river to me. It sounds like that river must like little girls!"

"Do you think so?"

"Oh, I do. I don't think it would hurt you, Sarah. I think any river that would want to play by tickling you would never hurt you."

"That's good."

He caressed her forehead as she smiled at him. "Where did it tickle you? Does it like toes?" he asked.

Sarah giggled, "No, it doesn't like toes, Mr. Robert! It likes to tickle me here and here." Sarah's hands moved to the middle of her chest, then to either side of her head.

"When did it tickle you?"

"After I talked to Miss Snider it really tickled a lot. Then when Mr. Osbourne came in it tickled some more."

"That's very interesting, Sarah. Did it tickle when Mr. O'Brien came to visit you today?"

"Well, just a little bit." She looked at Robert, concern etched on her gaunt face. "Mr. Robert, what do you think it is?"

Parnell paused as he thought for a moment, then stroking her hair as he talked to her. "Sweetie, I think that river is part of that place called Heaven that your mommy told you about. And I think it comes and tickles you because it knows that you're full of Love, just like Heaven is. It comes to share its Love with you. There's no way it's going to hurt you, sweetheart. You don't have to be afraid of it."

"Does it mean that I'm going to die real soon?"

"No, Sarah, it doesn't mean you're going to die soon. I think it just means that you don't have to be afraid when it comes time for you to go to Heaven. I think that river is just trying to tell you that there is lots of Love waiting for you in Heaven."

"Like from my mommy, right?"

"Yes, Sarah, your mommy is waiting for you. I bet she has lots and lots of hugs and kisses saved up for you too!"

"I'll...I'll try not to be afraid any more Mr. Robert. I'll try to be brave."

"Sarah, you don't have to try to be anything except you. I think you're just perfect just the way you are."

Sarah reached up and embraced Robert again. "Thanks for coming to see me, Mr. Robert. I love you."

A tear ran down Robert's cheek. "I love you too, Sarah." He held her in his arms for several minutes, clearing his throat so he would be able to speak. "Well sweetheart, it's getting very late. You must be tired. How about trying to go back to sleep now?"

"Okay," she said as calm returned to her face, "Tell Mrs. Parnell that I love her."

"I'll tell her. She loves you too, Sarah."

Robert kissed her on the cheek. "Night, night."

"G'night."

Sarah buried her head into her pillow as Robert tucked the blankets in around her. "Can you come and visit another day soon, Mr. Robert."

"Guaranteed. I'll be back next week and the week after that, and the week after that."

"Promise?"

Robert put his hand over his heart. "Scout's honor."

Sarah smiled and closed her eyes. "Good," she said as she drifted back to sleep.

Robert felt a hand on his shoulder and turned to see Todd. "Come on, Robert, let's go downstairs. I put on some coffee."

The two men poured themselves a cup of coffee. They stood in the kitchen doorway at the base of the stairway in the main hallway. "How's Sarah doing physically?" asked Robert in a hushed voice.

"Her blood counts haven't looked good the past several weeks. She's lost quite a bit of weight...she's down to twenty-nine pounds."

"Twenty-nine pounds!" Robert felt a heaviness wash over him. "How long do you think she has left?"

Todd shook his head. "It's hard to tell, it could be a few months, or a few weeks. Even days. It all depends on whether she gets any kind of infection. Her blood counts are so low, something like that could put her over the edge very quickly."

Robert reached over and grabbed Todd's arm. "I want you to promise me that you'll let me know when...she's..." Parnell closed his eyes, fighting back tears and trying to regain his composure. He started over. "Todd, when the time comes Sarah's going to want me by her side. Joanne will know where I am at all times. You have to call Joanne and let her know, so she can get a message to me. I have to be here with Sarah."

Todd placed his hand over Robert's. "You know I'll do that, Robert. We'll make sure you have the chance to be here with Sarah."

"Thanks."

"When's your flight tomorrow?"

"Six-fifteen. I have a presentation at a conference tomorrow in Toronto. I'm on stage at eleven in the morning."

Todd glanced at his watch and winced. "Ouch! It's almost midnight now. Listen…do you want to sleep at my place tonight? I can run you over to the airport in the morning."

"Okay."

"Do you feel like getting an update on how the project is going here?"

"Sure."

"The weighing equipment was calibrated yesterday, we're going to do final testing on it tomorrow."

"Pearce is okay with everything here?"

"Yes. Bill was in about four days ago with the video recorders and got that equipment all set up and running properly. The heart and brain wave monitors are already installed, tested and fully operational. Since we're not expecting any snags with the weighing equipment we should be up and ready to run by the day after tomorrow. How's it going in Toronto?"

"All of the installations have been completed ahead of schedule. Our final equipment test was earlier this week. From what Joanne told me we're ready now," Parnell explained.

"How about Pearce and Lopez in Los Angeles?"

"Bill and Dina figure they're no more than a week from test and start up." Parnell put his right hand on Todd's shoulder. "Well my friend, it's just about time. We're all going to find out where this journey is going to take us." He tilted his head back and looked up the stairwell toward Sarah's room, his voice wavering as he spoke. "We have to help our little angel find her way back home."

CHAPTER 18

The next morning Todd dropped Robert off at the airport then continued on to his office to get caught up on some paperwork. About seven-thirty he dialed Stephanie's telephone number and was greeted by a sleepy Laura Snider.

He recognized her voice. "Good morning sleepyhead."

She yawned, "Todd? What time is it?"

"Seven-thirty. Is Stephanie at home?"

"No, she has a morning shift."

"What did she say about helping out at Winterhaven?"

"She thinks she'll be able to cover two or three shifts a week."

"Fabulous. Did Greg get a hold of her yet?"

"I don't think they have connected. He left a message on her answering machine."

"It would be great if she volunteered. It would ease some of the scheduling pressure that Greg's had to deal with at Winterhaven lately. What time does your flight to Los Angeles leave today?"

"Around two o'clock."

"If you haven't made other arrangements I'd like to take you to the airport."

"I'd like that."

"Great. I got into the office early today so I can spring a good portion of the morning open. How would you like to spend your last morning in Chicago having brunch with me?"

"Sounds wonderful."

"Once you get packed up I can meet you at Stephanie's."

"Do you still have her address?"

"Yeah. How about if I pick you up around ten-thirty or eleven? I can have you to the airport in time for your flight."

"It's a deal. See you at ten-thirty."

Laura put the telephone down as a feeling of relief swept over her. By ten-fifteen she was packed and ready. Within ten minutes she saw Todd's car pull into the driveway of the condominium. She grabbed her bags and headed for the elevator so she could meet him in the lobby.

As she exited the elevator she could see him pressing the apartment buzzer. He happened to glance over as she was walking across the foyer, smiling and spreading his arms wide. He was barely audible through the glass.

"So there you are. I thought you had changed your mind."

Laura flicked the locking mechanism on the door and opened it, laughing, "And what would make you think that I would change my mind? You know that I'm the kind of girl that can't pass up a free meal."

Todd flicked his eyebrows up and down. "Well, at least I now understand your motivation." He helped carry her luggage out to his car then they headed off to the restaurant, arriving just after eleven.

After filling their plates at the buffet, they found a table that looked out over the bustling street.

"I love watching people, " said Todd, "I always wonder what their stories are. Where they've been. What they've done. What kind of dreams they have for the future."

Laura gazed out of the window. "I guess I've never paid that much attention to other people. I've always been too wrapped up in my own life," she said looking at Todd, "You must think that's terribly selfish."

He shrugged his shoulders. "We all have our moments, Laura. It's pretty hard for any of us not to focus on our day to day struggles."

"Do you remember the night we went out to Tony Ambruzzo's for a pizza?"

"Sure."

"You said something that upset me at the time and I never gave you a chance to explain. Do you remember?"

"It would be hard to forget. You asked me what I saw when I looked at you and I said a contradiction. Then you got really defensive with me."

"That's right I did. Why did you say that I was a contradiction?"

"Well, I guess I sensed some polarized things in you. A street wise women with an undercurrent of vulnerability. A hard bargainer with a streak of generosity. A cynic with an element of compassion. There seemed to be sides of you that were very different from what you showed the world."

"I think we all do that to some extent. I haven't met many bartenders with a Ph.D."

"I'd like to say that my bartending is purely a magnanimous gesture, an attempt to offer professional advise to the down-trodden of the world, but that would be a lie. What my part time job really does is keep me in touch with middle and senior managers of corporations from all across North America. Many will open up to a bartender and talk about their frustrations and fears. They'll talk about how problems are handled within a company and what happens as a result. These insights allow me to better understand what some of the management and interpersonal issues are in corporations today and it gives me a better chance to develop programs that will work in the real world."

"So, we finally get to see the pragmatic businessman side."

Todd smiled warmly, "Well, at some point we all come face to face with reality, the need to put a meal on the table and a roof over our head."

Laura's gaze drifted back out to the street. "I was relieved this morning when you called."

"Why?"

"Because I wanted to see you again before I left for Los Angeles, but I was afraid to call you."

"Why would you be afraid?"

Snider looked down at her plate, moving some of the food with her fork. "I…I feel things inside when I'm around you that I've never felt before. I don't feel I can control what's happening," she said looking up at him, "Being out of control brings back painful memories. It scares me."

He reached over and held her hand. "I won't push you, Laura. I'll be as close as you want me to be, but it's up to you to decide."

"I guess that's what scares me. I wonder what you'd really do if I made a decision to try and make something of us. Could you ever get over...my..."

"Your past?"

"Yes." Laura's eyes were wide and moist. "I really want to believe that."

"What could I do to help convince you?"

"I don't know."

Todd peered out over the street as he thought, his lips drawing tight. He looked back at Laura. "When I was working on my Ph.D. I had a chance to do some fieldwork and one of the things I did was spend some time with inmates at a facility for the criminally insane. There were about thirty-five or forty men in the section I was working in. Between them they had probably committed eighty or ninety murders and several hundred rapes."

Todd winced as he remembered. "Some of the crimes were horrific." He paused to collect himself. "The men that I was dealing with had been through years and years of therapy and all of them had a lot of work left to do if they were to have any hope of ever getting out. The one thing that really struck me was how normal most of them seemed. I realized that they were exactly the same as me."

Snider studied him intently watching as he extended his hands, palms facing her as if he was pressing them against an invisible wall.

"I realized the only thing that separated their lives from mine was an ultra thin membrane of restraint. For whatever reason something had happened inside of them that made them break through that membrane, if only for an instant. What they were capable of when they crossed over can't be described."

140

Todd brought his hands together as if in prayer. "Laura, that fleeting moment, when they crossed through that membrane and I didn't, was the only thing that made my life different from theirs. I came to understand that none of us can ever say what we would do, or not do, in a given situation. None of us really knows what we are capable of doing until the moment is upon us. I couldn't judge any of those men for what they did and I can't judge you."

Snider's head was cocked to one side, studying him intently, "So what do we do?"

"Let's just focus on where we are right now, and where we want to be in the future."

"I'll try if you will."

O'Brien nodded his agreement, "Good. I think that's enough for now. We can move on when you're ready."

They continued with their meal and found that their conversation rambled over many topics, eventually coming to Robert Parnell.

"Did I tell you that I saw Robert speak at the convention centre a couple of days after you and I went to Tony Ambruzzo's?"

"Uh-huh. What did you think of Robert?"

"He made me think about things in ways I never had before."

Todd smiled, "I know that feeling first hand."

"One of the things that he asked the audience to think about was why each of us picked our parents. I thought it was a really bizarre question. Especially given my childhood."

O'Brien looked quizzical. "What made your childhood different?"

Laura stared out of the window to the street below. "Other than my father raping me repeatedly, probably not much."

Todd's eyes narrowed, his stomach knotted. "What?"

"It's okay, Todd. That was a long time ago and he's dead now anyway. Robert said that if we could figure out why we picked our parents we'd never have to be a prisoner to the past. When I heard him say that at the convention centre that night it struck a chord deep inside me. It was as if no one else in the hall even existed. It felt that he was speaking directly to me. I thought if I could understand why I picked my father, then maybe I could finally get rid of the hurt."

He reached out and held her hands, "And were you able to do that, Laura?"

"Not by myself. Sarah helped me."

"Sarah?"

"That's why I was crying when we left Winterhaven. We were talking in her room about her mom, and mine, about her dad, and how she didn't know him much. Suddenly I found myself talking to her about what my father did to me. Imagine talking to a little girl and telling her about your father raping you."

"What was Sarah's reaction?"

"She seemed to understand the pain and the shame I felt. Then she looked at me and said that she thought I must be very brave and strong to be able to tell her about it."

"How did that make you feel?"

"How would that make anybody feel? Here I am sitting on the side of the bed of a fragile, little, seven-year-old girl who's dying of AIDS. A little girl who hasn't given me the faintest hint of feeling sorry for herself. I can almost see her life ebbing away in front of me and she tells me that she thinks I'm brave, that I'm strong. I guess for the first time in my life, I felt lucky to be alive. Lucky to have more life ahead of me. I realized that I am a survivor." Tears were welling up in her eyes.

"So, did you figure out why you picked your father?"

"As Sarah and I continued to talk, I realized that I had been trying to punish my dad, for what he did to me, by what I was doing to myself. I realized that I was letting him control me, even from his grave. Then I thought about the power I feel when I've got some guy panting and sweating for my body. How I can play him like a fish hooked on a line, and squeeze more money out of him. It's so easy." Laura looked at her hands intertwined with Todd's. "And, it's so easy to lose yourself in that feeling of power. Like how my dad was lost in the power he had over me, and how I've been lost in the power I've had over the men who pay me."

"That's what I learned Todd, that control is just an illusion. You think you have it but it has you. Power is a drug. It's a drug we use when we're empty inside and we don't know who we are, and where we're going. Power is the ultimate attempt we make to fill the hole that's inside of us. But afterwards, when we've used that power, the emptiness inside of us still aches. I've learned that when we need power, we become its prisoner and we become a stranger to ourselves."

"So, where do we go from here, Laura?"

"I can't just jump over the edge with you right now Todd. It's too frightening."

"I understand that. There's no need to rush this."

"I'd like to look at today as a fresh start and take some baby steps from here."

CHAPTER 19

After Todd dropped Laura off at the airport he returned to his office and checked for messages. There was a particularly emotional one from Joanne Parnell. He called her back immediately.

"Joanne, I got your message. What's up?"

"I wanted to let you know that our first patient has been moved into the Transporter Room in Toronto. He went in at about three-thirty this morning."

"How are the other patients reacting?"

"They're all very apprehensive which is a little surprising since the mood has been so positive since this whole thing started."

"But don't forget that this is the first real test of the project. They'll all be on pins and needles until those first results are known."

"You're right. They're looking for proof like everyone else. I'm afraid if the tests don't show what we've been looking for the other volunteers will back out."

"Well, that's a risk we knew that we'd have to take. We knew from the start this endeavor might end up a total failure. Did Robert get back into town in time for his presentation?"

"Yes, but he didn't have too much time to spare. He was a little concerned he didn't have as much time as he would have liked to get himself ready. You know what a perfectionist he is. He always wants to give a hundred percent. I'm expecting him home in another couple of hours."

"Does he know about the Transporter Room in Toronto?"

"Yes. I had a chance to tell him when he called from the air-port after he landed this morning."

"What was his reaction?"

"Quiet confidence. He seems to know that everything is going to work out. I wish I was as confident."

"What's going to happen is what's going to happen, Joanne.

We can't control that. All we can do is accept the roles the Universe has handed us. How's the patient in the Transporter Room?"

"Quiet and stable. Some of the other patients are taking turns trying to comfort him."

"Is there any family present?"

"No. His family disowned him years ago when they found out that he was gay. We did contact them but they wouldn't talk and refused to visit."

"All we can do is try and keep him as comfortable as possible, give him as much emotional support as we can, and wait. I know that sounds cold, but that's the reality of the situation."

"I know that intellectually. It's the emotional side that is so tough. How can people be so cruel and hard-hearted? How can they turn their backs on others, especially a family member? I just don't understand it."

"I don't know either Joanne. We can only do what we can to let him know that he is loved. That he has intrinsic human value that nothing can diminish or take away."

"How are things going in Chicago?"

"We're doing our final equipment testing this morning, so we could be ready to go later today if needed. Things in California seem to be doing very well too."

"That's my understanding. When I talked to Robert he said that Bill and Dina are really working well as a team."

"Robert told me that they should have the Los Angeles facility ready within the week. My friend Laura has volunteered her time to the project," Todd replied.

"Robert will be very happy to hear that."

"She left for L.A. this afternoon." O'Brien paused for a moment. "What's your read on Robert these days?"

"You mean how he's reacting to Sarah's condition?"

"Yes."

"There's something deep inside that's tearing him apart.

In all the years I've known him he's always been able to stand back from life's dark moments and somehow find a broader meaning."

"I know. It's one of his great gifts."

"This time he just can't do it. Whenever he thinks about Sarah's illness, he gets bitter. I've never heard him complain before about life not being fair, but he does when he thinks of her."

"That's strange for Robert. Over the years he's told me numerous times that the Universe always sends us the message we need, when we need it, and that our challenge is to be open to receive it regardless of the form it comes in."

"He knows that, but he has such a strong connection with Sarah that he can't stand back from it. How is she?"

"Not good. She's lost another couple of pounds since Robert was last here, and her blood counts have continued to fall."

"You have to let me know when she goes into the Transporter Room. Robert just has to be there for her."

"I've already made arrangements with Greg Osbourne. He's posted instructions on the staff bulletin board at Winterhaven and he'll be holding meetings with all the volunteers. The moment Sarah goes into the Transporter Room the shift supervisor will call all of us; me, you, and my friend Laura in California. Sarah's touched us all and we all want to be there for her."

"Thanks Todd. Hopefully we won't get that call for some time yet."

✳

After finishing his conversation with Joanne, Todd went to some client meetings for the balance of the afternoon returning to the office shortly after five o'clock to get caught up on some paperwork. He looked at the stacks of paper and file folders waiting for him on his desk and at the stack of yellow telephone message slips, thinking, "I swear paper must come in male and female. It seems whenever I'm away it propagates."

By eight o'clock he was ready to call it quits and started to re-stack some of the folders. The telephone rang. Todd glanced at his watch as he answered it, wondering who would be calling after regular business hours.

"Todd! It's Joanne. We've...we've...the Transporter Room!" She was breathless.

"Settle down, Joanne. What's happened with the Transporter Room?"

"He left us! Our patient left us! The auditors are here with the volunteer doctor."

"Does the family know?"

"Yes. We called them right away."

"Are they okay?"

"Hard to tell. We got no reaction from them over the telephone, and they still refused to come to the hospice."

"What did they auditors find?"

"Four-point-six! They found an instant weight loss of four-point-six ounces at the moment when both brain and heart activity stopped."

"Have the auditors verified that yet?"

"That's what they're doing right now. They're examining all the seals on the video equipment and the recording grid."

"When will they be able to confirm the findings?"

"Pretty soon I think. Probably within the next half hour or so. Todd, this place is going nuts. One of the patients overheard the doctor reading the results on the recording paper. News spread like wildfire! You can't believe the attitude of all the patients here!"

"Joanne, try and get them calmed down. We need to wait until the auditors have reviewed everything so that there's no possibility of a mistake. We can't afford to let this thing get out of control. We have to make sure we have the findings verified and get the auditors to sign off on the control sheets."

"I'll do what I can."

"Is Robert there?"

"No, he's on his way over. He was really tired after the early morning flight and the presentation today so he laid down for a nap after dinner. I called him a little while ago. Do you want me to have him call you when he arrives?"

"Have him call me when you know what the auditors found. I'll order in a pizza and wait for his call here at the office."

Todd put the telephone down, and sat on the edge of his desk, feeling overwhelmed with emotion. He unfastened the top two buttons on his shirt and reached in for the medallion hanging around his neck. As he held the medallion in his hand tears welled up in his eyes. Visions of his father flashed through his mind. His stomach was churning with emotion so Todd decided not to order a pizza and paced the office for over an hour instead, waiting for Robert to call.

When the telephone rang he pounced on it before it had the chance to ring a second time.

"Hello! Robert?"

"Yes, Todd."

"What did the auditors find?"

"They've signed off on it, Todd. They've signed off on a documented case of a four-point-six ounce weight loss at the moment of physical death. The auditors' report will show death defined as the cessation of recorded heart and brain function."

"Did the attending physician sign off as well?"

"Yes. Everything is documented and signed exactly as we planned. The auditors have reviewed the split screen master videotape. They've certified that the seals on the video equipment were original."

Todd felt the tension drain from his body. "It's been a long journey, Robert."

"It's not over yet. This is just one documented case. The medical and scientific communities will need more than just one case before they'll even think about listening to us."

"You're right. I should have remembered that from my university studies. We'll need at least fifty, probably a hundred documented cases without even the smallest glitch before they'll pay any attention."

"That's going to take at least a couple of months, maybe more, before we're in a position to go public with this."

"That sounds like it might be extremely difficult to do. Joanne was saying that the hospice up there was in a real state of turmoil when she called earlier."

"That's why I couldn't call you earlier. I was trying to get everybody here calmed down. It was absolute bedlam for a while! I explained to the rest of the patients how important that it is that we not go public with our findings until we're ready. I impressed on them how critical it is for us to have a large enough sample base to make our findings legitimate."

"What was their reaction?"

"Once I got them calmed down it went very, very well. They all understood the need to maintain a sense of composure through this process. You should have felt the energy in the room. It was unbelievable! I think they all know that they're a part of something monumental. The positive attitude and commitment was remarkable."

"Do you really think we'll be able to keep a lid on this?"

"In all honesty, I don't have a clue," Parnell replied.

"Has anyone talked to Bill and Dina?"

"Joanne called them a little while ago. Both were really excited by the news. I'm going to call them again later just to reinforce the need to keep a low profile on this until we have more documented cases."

"Did they mention whether they had a chance to meet with Laura today?"

"They met a couple of hours before Joanne called. Bill didn't say much other than Laura was very receptive to helping out any way she could. Todd, we called Winterhaven earlier but I missed Greg. Can you call him and bring him up to speed."

"Sure, I've got his home number and I'll call him after we're done."

"Maybe you could go to Winterhaven tomorrow and meet with the patient volunteers. They should be made aware of what's happened and they also need to understand how important keeping a low profile is the next few months."

Todd flicked through the pages in his daily planner. "I'll change a couple of appointments in the morning. Shouldn't be any problem getting those things done tomorrow. Is there anything special you want me to tell Sarah?"

"Tell her that Joanne and I love her. I'm doing six back-to-back presentations out west starting late next week. Joanne's arranged for me to connect through Chicago on my way out and coming home. The travel agent arranged long stopovers on both legs so I'll have time to drop in for a visit with her. Let her know that I'll be coming in to see her just like I promised."

CHAPTER 20

The next morning, word of the results spread with lightning speed throughout the hospice test facilities in all three cities. Parnell, O'Brien, Pearce, Lopez and Osbourne quickly learned that they had to be concerned about more than just the three hospices with the Transporter Rooms. Word had leaked and all of the other hospices that had originally agreed to cooperate in the project were also in an uproar. The team quickly scheduled a series of meetings in Chicago, Los Angeles and Toronto, at all of the other cooperating facilities. They spent all day and evening conducting meetings across each of the three cities. In each case they pleaded with the patients to keep a low profile until more documentation could be gathered.

The team also reviewed each of the three main facilities to ensure that each Transporter Room was secure and afforded its occupant privacy. Osbourne and the others hadn't anticipated such an overwhelming reaction from the patients. The more the patients got excited about the project, the greater the risk of the media getting involved before the team had gathered sufficient data. The team was concerned about the project being turned into a circus event.

Osbourne decided to dedicate the entire third floor of Winterhaven to the Transporter Room. The only patients allowed on the third floor were Sarah and the Transporter Room occupant. Even though she hadn't exhibited any additional luminous body symptoms, Greg was concerned about such an occurrence and the effect it might have on the rest of the patients. He ordered two beds relocated to the other two floors, making the facility even more cramped.

The quick response of the team met with some success. In the meetings they had been able to convert the patients' excitement into a commitment to the project. There had also been one unexpected benefit from the rush of excitement; the project now had a tremendous pool of patient volunteers for the

Transporter Rooms. In fact, there were sufficient volunteers that the team now anticipated having their first one hundred documented cases within the first three months of operation.

Over the next eight days the facilities in Chicago and Toronto were each able to document one patient departure every two or three days. The Los Angeles facility had been operational for the past four days. The results from across the continent were identical; a four-point-six ounce weight loss at the exact moment that brain and heart activity stopped. The auditor and medical verifications were completed without incident for each patient. The team was growing increasingly confident since they now had consistent results for nine cases.

Robert flagged a taxi as he stood outside the terminal building at O'Hare.   He was on his way to Winterhaven to visit Sarah as he had promised. Robert was starting his western speaking tour and after his stop over in Chicago he was headed to Los Angeles to speak at a large sales convention.

After an uneventful taxi ride and greeting Osbourne, Robert immediately went upstairs to the third floor to see Sarah. She was awake when he arrived and greeted him with a huge smile and outstretched arms, Robert embracing her at bedside.

"How's my little pumpkin today? I've really missed you Sarah!"

"I missed you too, Mr. Robert. I'm okay, but I like to sleep a lot now."

He looked at the frail figure in front of him. She had patches of raw skin on her elbows and on the back of her legs. Sarah had developed bedsores that wouldn't heal because of her weakened condition and her damaged immune system. Robert noticed her wince in pain as she tried to move.

"Why don't you stay still sweetie then it won't hurt. How about a game of Connect 4? I've been practicing."

"It's on the table like the last time."

Robert retrieved the game from the table and set it up on the edge of her bed. "Do you want the red pieces or the black ones?"

"Black."

"Okay. Be prepared to get beaten!"

Sarah's initial giggles were soon silenced as any significant movement of her body caused extreme discomfort. Robert watched, sharing in her agony. He suggested that she simply tell him where to put her pieces, but Sarah would have none of it. She was determined to play the game the way they had the day they first met. After completing the second game, it was obvious to Robert that Sarah was growing tired.

He caressed her forehead. "Well, it's plain to see that I need more practice since I still can't beat you. Would you mind if I put the game away now?"

"No. That's okay."

"It would be nice to just talk for a while." As Robert put the game pieces away Sarah began a series of deep, hacking coughs. He waited for her to settle before continuing their conversation.

"So what do you think about what's been going on around here lately, Sarah?"

"You mean the people going into the Transporter Room?"

"Sure. What do you think about that?"

"Well, I think the people staying here are more happy now. They don't seem to be so mad at each other."

"What do you mean? People were mad at each other? Do you mean that they were fighting?"

"No, I think they were scared. People treat each other kind of mean when they get scared. Anyway, they don't seem to be so afraid to go in there." Sarah pointed to the Transporter Room door.

"Do you think that's good?"

"Uh-huh. It's like you told me on the tape Mr. Robert. There's nothing that's going to hurt me when I leave. So, we don't have to be scared."

"That's right, Sarah. Have you made me a tape yet?"

"No, not yet. But I will someday."

"That would be very nice. Do you still remember how to

do it?"

He smiled as Sarah explained each step in detail. "Boy, are you ever smart! I didn't think you'd remember all those things you have to do, but you did!"

Sarah's face beamed with pride. "I told you that I'd remember! And see…the tape machine still looks brand new! I've been taking good care of it. Just like I said I would."

Robert smiled warmly at the huge eyes staring up at him. "I knew you would, Sarah. You're not just any little girl. A special little girl like you would always keep a promise."

Sarah nodded her agreement.

"Has your river come to play since the last time I was here?"

"Not very much. Sometimes, late at night when I wake up and there's nobody here, it comes and tickles."

"It still doesn't like toes?"

She giggled, "No, it doesn't like toes!"

"So, it comes to tickle you. As much as when you spoke to Miss Snider?"

"No, not that much."

"Why do you think your river comes to play?"

"I don't know."

"Was there anything special that happened when Miss Snider came to see you? Your river must have really liked her visit."

"It tickled a lot after Miss Snider was here." Sarah thought for a few moments before she continued. "I think the river was happy and wanted to play because when Miss Snider left she was very happy."

"Was Mr. Osbourne happy? The river tickled then, too."

"No, he wasn't happy. He looked scared."

"Hmm. I wonder why the river would tickle you when Mr. Osbourne was here then?"

"Well, I was thinking about how happy Miss Snider was, even when Mr. Osbourne came in. You like to talk about my river don't you Mr. Robert?"

"Yes, I do Sarah."

"Why?"

"Because I think it's a very special place. And only very special people like you have a chance to see it."

"Have you seen it, Mr. Robert?"

"No, I haven't. That's why I like it when you tell me what it looks like and what it does. That way I can learn from you."

"Why haven't you seen it yet?"

"I don't know, Sarah. Maybe the river doesn't want me to see it yet."

"But you're nice, I don't know why the river wouldn't let you see it."

"I don't know why either."

"Maybe I could help you see it!"

Robert stroked her head, "Maybe you will, sweetheart. Maybe you will."

"Why do you think my river comes and tickles me, Mr. Robert?"

"I think it comes to tickle you because it wants to share its Love with you. I think it comes to visit you when your thoughts have Love in them. When you think about people you love."

"When I wake up in the night sometimes I think about my mother and it tickles." Sarah was very pensive. "Mr. Robert, I get a lot more tired than I used to when I first came here. I heard other people talking. They said that when you get really tired it means you're going to die pretty soon."

"I don't know, Sarah."

"I do. I think I'm going to die pretty soon. My body hurts a lot now and it didn't before."

Robert fought back his tears, "Sarah, just remember that the hurt is going to go away when you see your mommy again."

"I listen to the tape you gave me every day, Mr. Robert. I know my mommy is waiting for me. I know she's going to give me hugs and kisses when she sees me again."

CHAPTER 21

Robert's mind was full of images of Sarah as his airplane was en route to Los Angeles. After speaking to Greg, he realized that Sarah was right; she was nearing the end. Her body had little strength left to fight a lung infection that was making it difficult for her to breath.

He had called Joanne from the airport in Chicago and had given her the news about Sarah, both weeping openly.

Robert was finding it difficult to concentrate on his series of west coast presentations. His schedule would take him from Los Angeles to San Francisco, then on to Denver. From Denver he was to fly back to Los Angeles for another presentation, then go north to Vancouver, British Columbia. He would end the six event tour in Scottsdale. Rather than review his presentation Robert decided to try and get some sleep on the flight. A few hours later the airplane began its descent into Los Angeles and Robert began to wake as a stewardess shook him gently.

"Sir, sir, you need to put your seat upright. We're beginning our final approach."

Robert looked out over the sprawling metropolitan area and thought about his flight to L.A. when he first met Bill Pearce, their conversation about concurrent existence playing back through his mind. He smiled as he remembered the expression of disbelief on Bill's face, and hearing his promise to help if Robert could devise a way to prove the existence of this second energy realm. Now the project was well underway, with exciting early results. It was hard to believe so much had happened in such a short time. Robert was looking forward to seeing Bill again to thank him personally for his contributions to the project. It would also be the first time he'd have the chance to meet Dina Lopez. Robert gazed out of the window as he felt the familiar bump of touchdown.

After picking up his bags, Robert hailed a cab to take him to his hotel. At hotel check-in he was handed an urgent message from Todd that sent him rushing to his room. After tossing his bags on the bed he called him.

"Todd, it's Robert. I just got in to the hotel here in Los Angeles and received your urgent message. What's up?"

"The damn media is up! They're at Lopez's facility right now! Bill Pearce is there, trying to help her deal with the situation. Apparently somebody with an axe to grind got wind of our project and tipped off the media. The local television station showed up with cameras and a crew and they have been trying to get into the facility. They're making it seem that we're some kind of weird cult playing mind games with dying AIDS patients."

Robert glanced at his watch. "Hang on a second while I put the television on." He grabbed the remote control and started flicking through the stations, suddenly seeing a familiar shape; the huge, bearded, bear-like Pearce. He was standing on the steps of the hospice in Los Angeles, blocking the media from entering.

"It's worse than that Todd. It's on local television right now." Robert felt his heart sink as he watched the live coverage. The reporter, having been refused entry into the facility, was broadcasting live from the scene. Robert turned up the volume on the television with the hopes that Todd would be able to hear it.

"And so ladies and gentlemen since we can't get into this facility, it seems that this strange experiment will stay a mystery a little while longer. What you see behind me is the hospice in Los Angeles that is supposedly linked to some kind of experiment with dying AIDS patients. We understand that there are similar experiments going on in Chicago and Toronto, Canada. All we've been able to find out is that the people running these facilities are, get this, trying to prove the existence of the soul by monitoring the weight of AIDS patients at the moment of death. In fact, our sources say that they've pegged the weight of the soul at four-point-six ounces. Well, this is sunny, southern California, home to all kinds of nut bars! All you fad dieters better be careful, the next four-point-six ounces you lose could be your soul! For channel seven news…this is Steve Thompson."

Robert turned off the television. "Did you catch that Todd?"

"Yes. What should we do next?"

"I'll call Joanne and ask her to call our publicist. If there's a way to minimize the damage from this Marsha will know what to do. The most important thing is what effect it will have on the patient volunteers."

"I don't think we'll know about that until the morning."

"Let's talk tomorrow."

Robert hung up the telephone and dialed his home number, Joanne answering on the second ring.

"Robert, I've heard what's happening in Los Angeles."

"How?"

"It's on the television news here so I called Marsha a few minutes ago. I figured she'd know what we should do next from a public relations standpoint."

"What did she say?"

"Marsha feels the best strategy is to open up to the media. If we tell them what we're doing, the results we've measured so far, and the rationale behind it we might be able to negate the damage from today's coverage. Worst case, if we can't fix the damage from today, is that media would have had their feeding frenzy with us and will move on to other stories tomorrow."

"Do you agree with her?"

"Yes, I do. The approach does have risks, but I think it's better than trying to avoid the press which would only make them more suspicious."

"Okay, let's do it."

"I'll call her back right away and get more details on how she'd recommend we handle this. Robert, are you okay?"

He sighed, "Yeah, I suppose we knew last week that this was a possibility. At least we've got a small test sample to discuss with the media. I just hope this news coverage doesn't hurt the patients in the hospices across the continent. They're in enough pain and they so desperately need a sense of comfort. They need to know that this other realm exists so," suddenly the words from Osbourne's letter came back to him "…when it comes time to leave this world, they can do so the same way they entered it. In dignity and without fear."

"I love you Robert. I'll get a hold of Marsha." Joanne hung up the telephone, quickly dialing the publicist's number.

✱

Within the hour Robert received a call from his publicist. She detailed the strategy to deal with the media: Parnell would call the station and invite them to the hospice for a tour of the facility. Parnell, Lopez and Pearce would hold a press conference, answering all questions put to them and giving the media their full cooperation. The station would be free to have experts accompany the reporter and camera operators on the facility tour.

Robert called Dina Lopez and Bill Pearce at the hospice and explained the strategy to them. Pearce was not very comfortable with the strategy, expressing his concerns over the speakerphone, "Robert, you don't know what the media is like here in Los Angeles. This is a pretty jaded town. We could get eaten alive!"

"Better to get eaten alive than run away and hide. I'm proud of what we're trying to do. I'm proud of all the patients who have volunteered to help us, and I'm proud of all the people on our teams in Los Angeles, in Chicago, and in Toronto. I don't see that we have much choice."

"Okay Robert, if that's what you think we should do we're with you one hundred percent," said Pearce.

Dina spoke up, "Let's set it up as early tomorrow as we can. I'll stay here at the hospice tonight and tell everyone what's going on. If anybody is uncomfortable dealing with the media we should give them the chance of leaving the facility. I'll call the other hospices in the area and ask them to make temporary room."

After he got off the telephone Robert took the directory out of the desk drawer and flipped through it until he found the number for the television station. He took a deep breath and punched in the ten digits, and waited for the receptionist to answer.

"Channel seven news, the eyes of L.A."

"Steve Thompson, please."

"Yes, sir. May I say who is calling?"

"Robert Parnell. You can mention to Mr. Thompson that I'm calling about the hospice story he broadcast earlier today."

"One moment, sir."

Robert felt the dryness in his mouth and tried to swallow to clear his throat as he waited for Thompson.

"Newsroom. Steve Thompson."

"Mr. Thompson, it's Robert Parnell calling. Could we discuss your story about the hospice?"

"Not much to discuss since your folks wouldn't let us in."

"We're not trying to keep anything from the media, it's just that..."

Thompson cut Robert off in mid sentence. "Sure, and that's why your bearded mountain man was so cooperative today."

"That was a bit of a misunderstanding."

"Yeah, right."

Robert paused to collect his thoughts. "If you don't mind I'd like to start this conversation over. Would you mind if I called you Steve?"

"No problem...Bob," Thompson replied with an edge.

"Steve, we've got quite a few patients who have volunteered to help us with our research. We didn't feel it was ethical for us to allow your crew into the facility and compromise our patients' confidentiality. That's the only reason we didn't let your crew in."

"You're saying you'd be willing to let us into the facility?" Thompson replied skeptically.

"Absolutely. We just want to be able to let the patients

choose whether they want to be in the facility when your crew visits. We'd be happy to give you a tour and answer any questions you may have about the project."

"On camera?"

"Yes."

"When?"

"Tomorrow morning if you like. We'd also encourage you to bring any medical or scientific experts you'd like to have along."

"What's the catch?"

"No catch. Just the truth."

"Hang on a minute." Thompson scanned the crew assignments for the next morning then called out across the newsroom. "Hey, Jamie! Can I get a mobile unit and shooter for the morning to do a follow up on the hospice story?"

The assignment editor signaled his agreement.

"Okay, you're on. We'll see you in the morning between nine-thirty and ten."

Robert called Lopez and Pearce, telling them about the planned follow up visit by the news crew and asking them to prepare the patients. Then he spoke to Joanne and briefed her about the plans for the morning. After picking at his dinner at the hotel restaurant, Robert tried to get some sleep so he'd be fresh when he faced Steve Thompson. He spent a fit-full night pacing the floor.

✳

The next morning Lopez, Parnell and Pearce greeted the television crew on the front steps of the hospice and led them inside. About half of the patients had decided to leave for the day and were moved to neighbouring facilities. After giving the media a general tour of the facility, Dina took them into the Transporter Room, Robert and Bill following them in.

Lopez had set up a small desk and several chairs in the room. She, Pearce and Parnell held a small press conference in the Transporter Room, answering all the questions posed to them and providing details of their research objectives, methodology, and verification procedures. Within twenty-five minutes it was over, with the camera operators packing up to leave, and the reporter, Steve Thompson, checking his notes.

"I have to thank you folks for being so open today. It's too bad we had to broadcast the story the way we did yesterday. You guys have to realize that whenever the media is shut out of something our natural instinct is to think there's something weird going on."

"That's all right, Steve," said Robert, "We weren't trying to hide anything. We just weren't ready for you."

"I appreciate that. I also appreciate the fact you let us come in here early today. It gives us a little time to do some more research on this story before we air the follow-up piece tonight."

As Thompson turned to leave he shook hands with the three of them. "I can't say that I necessarily believe in what you're doing here, but I certainly can't doubt your sincerity. Good luck. We'll see you on the six o'clock news."

"Thanks for getting everything ready this morning, Dina," said Robert, "I've got to get downtown for my presentation. I guess there's not much else we can do now except wait for the six o'clock news."

Before Pearce and Parnell left they went with Lopez and visited each of the patients who had decided to remain in the facility, thanking each one for their faith and support. Pearce pulled his car around to the front of the hospice as Robert was saying his farewell to Dina.

"Robert, let me give you a ride back to the hotel."

"That would be great, Bill."

Robert climbed into the front seat, both of them waving to Dina as they pulled away. Bill reached over and squeezed Robert's forearm.

"I want you to know that regardless of what happens I can't thank you enough for letting me be a part in this project."

"Thank me? You've done so much Bill."

"Remember our meeting on the flight to L.A.?"

"I was thinking about it as the airplane was landing yesterday."

"When you told me about concurrent existence, about being in two different energy dimensions at the same time. I must admit I thought I was speaking to a bit of a lunatic. But, the more we spoke the more I found myself being drawn into this adventure and the more I understood that I needed to play a part in this search."

"I don't know what we would have done without you, Bill."

"Robert, it's important for me to tell you this..."

"What?"

"Regardless of how this turns out, I want you to know that being involved with this project has changed my life. Ever since the first test results came in from Toronto I haven't been able to look at the world in the same way. I know what we've found! I know we've found that four-point-six ounces leave here and go somewhere else. It doesn't matter who else believes us. I *know*. Remember when you told me that a Universal truth cannot be completely understood unless people experience it for themselves?"

"I remember."

"Robert, when I got off that airplane after meeting you, I knew you would be calling me to ask me for my help, and I also knew that, regardless of what you asked me for, I had to say yes. I knew that the Universe was sending me a lesson through you and I had to take it."

"And something told me that you needed to be a part of this too."

A tear snaked down Bill's cheek. He released Parnell's forearm so he could wipe it away. "I'll never forget this experience, Robert. Never."

"Neither will I, Bill."

The balance of the drive back to Robert's hotel was filled with discussion about the patients at the Los Angeles hospice, equipment maintenance and other project related subjects. The men embraced warmly as Bill dropped Robert off in front of the lobby entrance.

Before reviewing the material for his afternoon presentation, Robert called Joanne to tell her about the press conference, both agreeing that there wasn't much else they could do except wait for the six o'clock news broadcast. Robert began his presentation at the sales convention at two-thirty in the afternoon, wrapping up just before five o'clock. He signed autographs for another twenty-five minutes, returning to the hotel in time to watch the news at six o'clock. He sat on the edge of his bed and flicked on channel seven with the remote. The lead story was about the Los Angeles hospice, the segment opening with Steve Thompson, microphone in hand, on the front steps of the hospice.

"Tonight, ladies and gentlemen we have an in-depth follow-up on the story we brought you last evening about the hospice in Los Angeles that is taking part in an experiment to discover the weight of the soul. Earlier today we were invited back to the facility by Robert Parnell, the internationally recognized author and speaker. Also taking part in the follow-up interview were Dina Lopez, the hospice director and Bill Pearce, the owner of a Los Angeles based video production company who is also involved with this project."

After the introduction, portions of the taped media interview were shown, lasting for several minutes. Thompson then appeared back on camera with three expert witnesses, interviewing each in turn. The first verified that the test methodology was appropriate, and in fact, very well executed. The second guest was a prominent area physician who defined death in medical terms and supported the definition on the auditors' reports at the hospice. She also verified that the instrumentation used to measure heart and brain activity had been appropriately used. Robert's spirits soared.

The final expert guest was a Ph.D. physicist from the

University of Southern California. Steve Thompson ended the segment with this interview.

"We've seen a lot of compelling evidence to support the work that's being done at this hospice. Doctor, what's your expert opinion on the findings of this group?"

"There's nothing wrong with the research methodology or the verification process. Both are being done in a very professional manner. I see only one issue."

"What's that?"

"This entire experiment does nothing to prove the existence of the soul. All it does is verify an unexplained weight loss of four-point-six ounces at the time of death. Nothing more. Nothing less. Let's keep in mind that as human beings we've been terrified about the notion of death for thousands of years, so it's understandable that this group would try and interpret their findings in this manner. I have seen absolutely nothing that would lead me to believe that this unexplained weight loss has anything to do with the so called "energy of life" that Mr. Parnell spoke about earlier. Yes, they have proven that a weight loss occurs at the point of clinical death. That's all they have shown, that there is a weight loss. I reiterate, this does nothing to prove that the soul or any so-called 'energy of life' exists. I see nothing conclusive that actually supports their suggestion that this weight loss is directly linked with any specific energy associated with life as we know it."

Steve Thompson turned to face the camera. "Well, there you have it folks. Some well-intended research, by well-intended people, that unfortunately proves nothing. We're no closer to proving the existence of the soul than we have been for thousands of years. For channel seven in Los Angeles, this is Steve Thompson."

Robert turned off the television and headed for the bathroom as a wave of nausea swept over him.

CHAPTER 22

Before Robert left for San Francisco he called Steve Thompson to thank him for the media coverage the project had received. He didn't feel he could complain about the story since Thompson had tried to research the topic and present it in an unbiased fashion. The news segment had garnered international coverage, but unfortunately the comments from the physicist had proved damaging.

Robert had already heard from Joanne and Greg Osbourne and the reports had not been good. Both Winterhaven and the Toronto hospice had lost over seventy percent of their patient volunteers for the project. The news story had demoralized the bulk of the patients and even some of the facility volunteers had quit. There was a glimmer of hope; some of the facility volunteers, like Stephanie Mendoza, had taken on extra shifts to fill the vacant time slots and seemed to be even more committed to the project. Robert realized there wasn't much he could do until he returned from his western speaking tour and spent the next few days fighting back a deep depression.

Parnell's spirits picked up when he arrived in Vancouver. He had always liked the city and had spoken there on many occasions. Robert arrived at the hotel at ten-thirty, and after checking in, he went to the convention center across the street from the hotel to meet with the association's audio-visual support staff. Finding everything in good order he decided to go for a walk through Gastown.

Parnell enjoyed watching the double-decker tour buses negotiate their way through the crowded streets. He dropped into a number of the small shops along his route looking for a gift for Joanne, finally choosing a small soapstone carving. The smell of the salt water from Burrard Inlet filled his nostrils and fueled his hunger, so he stopped for a quick lunch. Soon he made his way back to the hotel to get ready for his presentation. After changing into a suit and tie he left for the convention center, failing to notice the message light blinking on the telephone in his room.

Robert's audience today was a national convention of real estate salespeople. He was scheduled to deliver a three-hour afternoon seminar, ending at four p.m. Parnell entered the hall just before one o'clock. Robert made his way to the vice-president of sales who was going to introduce him, and after exchanging some pleasantries, he took a seat just off to the side of the stage.

As Parnell was being introduced a meeting coordinator entered the hall and made her way quickly over to Robert. She handed him a note as he got up out of his seat and started moving toward the stage. The audience was already applauding his introduction when Robert glanced at the note. It was from Joanne.

"URGENT. Come to Chicago. Sarah went into the Transporter Room this morning."

Parnell stopped mid-way to the stage. Never in his twenty-two year speaking career had he ever been so compelled to walk out of a presentation. He stood there frozen, staring at the note. Gradually the applause subsided. Robert looked at the silent audience, the sea of eyes focused on him in anticipation. He took a deep breath and mounted the stage.

It took all of Robert's concentration to complete his afternoon program. During his presentation Parnell's emotions flowed like a torrent. The audience was totally mesmerized. After his presentation all seven hundred people in the audience rose in unison to give him a rousing ovation. He left the stage immediately and headed directly to the vice-president of sales who had introduced him. The man tilted his head so Parnell could speak into his ear, then they shook hands briskly, Robert immediately leaving the meeting room. The vice-president of sales took to the podium.

"Thank you Mr. Parnell for an incredible address. Ladies and gentlemen, due to a serious personal matter Mr. Parnell will not be able to sign autographs this afternoon. I know your hearts, like mine, are with him during this time of great need."

Robert ran to the elevator. When he got up to his room he threw his suitcase on the bed and stuffed his clothes into it. He grabbed the telephone and called the concierge. "Hello, this is Robert Parnell. I have a family emergency. I need a taxi for the airport. I'll be down in a minute."

He picked up his bags and ran out of his room to the elevator. After jabbing the elevator button half a dozen times, he looked up at the floor indicator lights, and seeing that all of the elevators were towards the top of the building he raced down the four flights of stairs down to the lobby rather than wait. As he passed the registration desk he gave his key and a business card to one of the clerks.

"I have an family emergency. Please send me the bill for my incidentals in the mail, and put the charges on my credit card imprint. Thanks."

As he approached the front door the concierge met him. "Mr. Parnell?"

"Yes."

"Your taxi is out front."

Robert tossed his bags into the back seat of the taxi, explaining his situation to the driver and handing him a fifty-dollar bill. The taxi screeched out of the parking lot and raced down the street.

Twenty-five minutes later Parnell was at the airport and very concerned. He could see thick fog rolling in from the ocean so he dashed into the terminal and went directly to the First Class check-in counter.

"I need to get to Chicago right away! I have a family emergency!"

"I'm very sorry sir, all the aircraft have been grounded."

"They can't be! I have to get to Chicago!"

"Sir, all the flights out of Vancouver were grounded about three hours ago because of the fog. At this point all of the flights for the next three to four hours have been cancelled. Looking at the conditions, there's a strong possibility that there won't be any more flights out today at all."

"I can't wait that long! I have to get to Chicago! You have to understand there's a little girl dying! I have to be there for her! Is there any way I can get to Chicago tonight?" Robert's mind raced, "Anything out of Seattle this evening?"

"Hold on a minute, sir." The reservations agent tapped a series of keystrokes on her computer. "You may be in luck. There's a flight that leaves SeaTac in four hours. The last report we had was that the fog wasn't extending too far south, so you may be able to drive to Seattle in time to make the flight. It will get you into Chicago before midnight."

"Can you get me on it?"

"Let me check for you. Do you have any luggage?"

"Just carry-on."

"Perfect. Let me see what we can do." After a series of keystrokes a smile broke over the agent's face. "We can get you on. Do you have a credit card handy?"

"Fantastic! Here's my credit card. I still need to rent a car."

"I understand." The agent quickly captured the required information and handed Robert's credit card back. "Rather than waiting for me to finish up this reservation why don't you go and get a rental car. When you come back I'll have your ticket printed."

"Thanks so much." Robert ran to the first car rental station that was open. "I need a rental car right away!"

"What size, sir?"

"I don't care! I just need a car right away. I have a family medical emergency! Can you get me one?"

"Yes, sir!"

He threw his driver's license and credit card down. "Get me a car, please! I need to drop it off at the airport in Seattle."

"There's an extra fee for that kind of drop off sir."

"It doesn't matter."

The agent worked quickly to issue the rental contract. As

Robert was signing the contract he asked for a map for Washington State and directions on how to get to SeaTac airport. Keys in hand, he returned to the First Class reservation agent.

She handed him a flight folder. "I have you confirmed on the next flight to Chicago out of SeaTac. It leaves in about four hours so you'll have to hurry. Your ticket and boarding pass are in this folder so you can go straight to the gate when you get there. Check in with the agent behind the counter."

"Thanks so much for your help!" He ran out to the rental car lot, finding his rental car quickly. He threw his bags in the back seat and roared out of the parking lot. Robert's heart was racing as he saw that the fog was starting to get thicker. He knew the reputation that Vancouver had for fog. He also knew that if he could get across the border quickly enough that, with some luck, he'd probably be able to make it to SeaTac in time for his flight.

Robert made good time getting to the US/Canada border crossing and within ten minutes he was across the border and heading south toward SeaTac. He didn't want to risk getting delayed because of a speeding ticket, so he set the car's cruise control for seven miles per hour over the posted speed limit, and stretched the map out over the passenger seat so he could monitor his progress.

He pulled into SeaTac thirty minutes before flight time, and after dropping his car at the quick return kiosk he ran into the terminal. He explained his plight to other passengers and was able to avoid the line-ups at security.

As Robert finally sunk into his seat on the Chicago bound jet he realized that he had forgotten to call Joanne to tell her that he was on his way. The only thing in his mind was a picture of Sarah.

✹

In a little more than three hours the jet was safely on the ground in Chicago. Parnell rushed out of the terminal and flagged a taxi. Another hefty tip sent the taxi speeding through the night toward Winterhaven.

The taxi screeched to a halt in front of the hospice. "Thanks so much!" Robert lunged out of the taxi and scurried up the steps into Winterhaven, dropping his bags and coat in the hall and ignoring everyone as he scrambled up the stairway to the third floor. He was met by a quartet of somber faces.

Robert stared at his wife, tears streaming down her face. "I'm sorry Robert. You're too late." Then he looked at Greg Osbourne, Todd O'Brien and Laura Snider. Their heads all hung low.

"No!" he screamed, "I can't be too late! I promised her!" He burst past them into the Transporter Room, finding Sarah's frail, lifeless body on the bed. A white sheet was pulled over her up to her chin. Parnell fell to his knees and pounded his fists on the floor, "No! No! No!" he sobbed.

Robert felt a familiar touch and looked up to see Joanne. "Come and sit on the side of the bed for a moment."

He gathered himself up and let Joanne guide him to a place on the side of the bed next to Sarah's body. She looked serene, at peace.

"Sarah knew that you were trying to be here with her, Robert. She knew you loved her. She played the tape you made for her and it gave her great comfort. I don't quite know how to say this, but she also gave you three gifts today."

Robert looked at his wife in total shock.

"Maybe I can explain."

Robert looked around to see Todd standing at the doorway to the Transporter Room.

"Robert, Sarah died four hours ago. We have everything recorded; her heart beat, her brain waves, her weight loss. It was four-point-six ounces like everyone else. It's all on the split screen video, just like everyone else. But she did something that no one else has done Robert. She did something that proves that the four-point-six ounces really is the weight of the energy of life, the soul."

"What did she do?" Robert asked incredulously.

"She came back. She was clinically dead for over an hour. We have it on the recording paper. We have it on time-coded video. We have it verified by the attending physician and the auditor. She was clinically dead and she came back. Sixty-three minutes later her weight jumped up by exactly four-point-six ounces. Her weight jumped up at precisely the same time her heart and brain began functioning again. Robert! The four-point-six ounces came back when she came back to life! We have it on the recording paper. We have it on time-coded video. We have it verified by the attending physician and the auditor. It's not just an unexplained weight loss anymore! We can relate the loss and *gain* of four-point-six ounces to life! To the energy of life!"

Robert was dumbfounded, looking at Todd in total disbelief.

Todd put both hands on his shoulders. "Robert, the split screen video has pictures of her coming back to life. She sat up in this bed and her body was glowing! Her entire body! She got up and went to the table to get the tape recorder you gave her and she taped a message for you. And after she taped the message, she reached for this pen on the nightstand. She removed the plastic tabs on the ends of the tape."

"Just like I showed her."

"Yes, Robert. Just like you showed her. Then she took out the marking pens and the paper you gave her and she wrote you a note, sealing it in one of the envelopes you bought for her. Then she lay back down on the bed and she left a second time. We have it all recorded; her brain waves, her heart beat, her loss of four-point-six ounces a second time. We have it all on split screen video. Robert, she came back to help you prove that there is an energy of life, a soul! She came back to help you prove that there is another place we all go!"

Robert sat in a state of amazement, "What did she say on the tape? What was the message she wrote on the paper for me?"

Joanne caressed the side of Robert's head. "We don't know. We didn't listen to the tape and we didn't open the envelope. They were gifts from Sarah to you. We saved them for you."

"Where are they?"

Joanne moved the sheet away from Sarah's body. Her right arm was draped over her chest, the audiotape and the envelope in her hand, both directly over her heart. Robert touched the little girl's hand and was stunned to find it still warm.

"The rest of her body shows all the usual signs of death, but her hand is still at normal body temperature. The doctors can't explain it," said Joanne. "She knew that you'd be here, Robert. She's been waiting for you to come and get your gifts."

Joanne and Todd left the room.

Robert grasped the right hand, finding it was warm and pliable. Sarah's hand immediately began to turn cold as soon as Robert removed the tape and envelop from its grasp. He looked at the label on the tape and smiled. 'A Gift from Sarah to Mr. Robert' was carefully printed on the label. He got up from the corner of the bed and walked over to tape player on the table. He pulled up a chair and sat down. Parnell put the cassette in the tape player, and pressed 'Play'. Sarah's voice filled the room.

Dear Mr. Robert,

This is a special gift for you. Just like I promised. I wanted you to know that you were right when you said that we can travel to this other place. We can, and it doesn't hurt when we leave our body behind, it just sort of tickles.

There is no time here because everything is Now. This place is a giant river of energy that is very beautiful. It shines all kinds of wonderful colours and there are no waves where I am. Everything is smooth and very warm. My mommy is here just like you said she would be. We are all a part of it and it is a peaceful place to be.

You need to tell people that if they want to live here when they leave their bodies behind, there are things they need to do everyday. To live in this beautiful part of the river, it doesn't matter what we said, or what we believed. It only matters what we did.

I left a note for you to give to people so they can ask themselves questions about how they live in their bodies. If they become the answers they need to live, they will learn how to get here too.

Mr. Robert, I know you weren't able to see this beautiful river before, but I know it will visit you now. It only tickles children so you will need to be strong because it is very powerful. You will be able to see it and touch it, and it will show you things you have never seen before. You need to share what you see with other people so you can help them find this river too.

A part of everyone is here in the river. It is hidden from us because it is us. When we are in our bodies we only sense being here and feel its wonders during special moments of Now. This river passes through everything, always, even where your body is right now. It always has.

Become Love, like it is Love, and it will touch you. Become Love, like it is Love, and it will wash over you. Become Love, like it is Love, and you will see the world through different eyes. Tell people about this river and give them the note so they can find their way here. It is Love and it is worth searching for.

I Love you Mr. Robert.
Sarah.

Robert turned off the tape recorder and looked at the sealed envelope in front of him. His fingers trembled as he opened it and removed a note written on a piece of the brightly coloured paper he had given Sarah.

Did we?

When we were given a day,
did we live it in joy and thanks?
When we were given talents,
did we use them to serve others?

When we were given sight,
> *did we see the world as a beautiful place?*

When we were given touch,
> *did we use it to comfort those in pain?*

When we were given a voice,
> *did we use it to encourage those that have fallen?*

When we were given ears,
> *did we hear the cries of those less fortunate?*

When we were given legs,
> *did we use them to travel to help a friend?*

When we were given a mind,
> *did we use it to create things of beauty?*

When we were given hands,
> *did we use them to build shelters for the poor?*

When we were given a strong back,
> *did we use it to help carry the weak?*

When we were given a heart,
> *did we fill it with compassion?*

When we were given Love, did we cherish every moment?
> *Did we give our Love freely to others?*

Tears streamed from Robert's eyes. He gently caressed the paper, his voice barely audible, "Thank you for all these gifts, Sarah. I will share them with other people just like you asked." A solitary tear dropped from his cheek, staining the note in his hand. He wiped the droplet away with his finger, surprised to find it hot to the touch.

Suddenly Robert felt the room begin to swirl around him. He closed his eyes and grabbed the seat of his chair in a desperate attempt to maintain his balance. His head was filled with a roar that sounded like cascading water. His jaws clenched as the vortex strengthened, its power almost lifting him up from the chair. He shuddered uncontrollably as searing daggers of pain shot up through his legs and arms. White-hot flashes of energy jabbed at his temples, and pulsed through his chest forcing his back to arch in agony. His body became rigid, head thrown back, mouth agape. A low, guttural moan escaped from his lips as he sank back in the chair.

Joanne's silhouette appeared at the doorway, a fist clenched to her chest. She stared at the motionless form of her husband, Sarah's note still in his hand.

"Oh God! Robert!"

The limp form began to move. As Parnell regained his strength he gathered himself and sat upright in the chair. As he turned to face her, Joanne gasped. Robert's eyes were glowing.

About the Author

Thomas Stirr is one of the founding partners of Rules of Engagement Inc., a training, development and consulting company that specializes in business development programs and personal effectiveness training. He speaks to corporations, public organizations, and community groups on a range of issues including leadership, relationship management, communications, and maximizing personal potential.

His first book, *Miller's Bolt: A Modern Business Parable* was published in the spring of 1997, and was subsequently produced in Spanish for the South American market. He has written numerous articles that have appeared in leading publications in Canada including Marketing Magazine, CMA Magazine, and Personal Success.

For more information about our keynotes, workshops, and seminars please refer to our web site:

www.rules-of-engagement-inc.com
Or email: tom@rules-of-engagement-inc.com

To contact:
Thomas Stirr

Write to:
Thomas-Ritt Associates Limited
P.O. Box 20055, 1 Main Street West
Grimsby, Ontario L3M 5J3 CANADA

Web site: www.4ouncestoheaven.com
Email: info@4ouncestoheaven.com